NIGHT
OF THE
DOGMAN
RETRIBUTION

LUKA T. JACOBS

Thank you to my family for their
unwavering support, with special gratitude
to the best father a girl could ask for.

FROM THE AUTHOR

Thank you for choosing my book as your next read. *"Retribution"* is the second installment in the *"Night of the Dogman"* series. The positive feedback from the first book, which also happened to be my debut novel, has been incredibly encouraging, and I felt compelled to continue the story with this sequel.

While *"Retribution"* can be enjoyed on its own, I highly recommend reading the first book to fully appreciate the characters and their backgrounds.

Thank you again, and happy reading!

Luka T. Jacobs

FB: **https://www.facebook.com/lukatjacobs**
A: **https://amazon.com/author/lukatjacobs**
W: **http://www.LukaTJacobs.com**

CONTENTS

PROLOGUE

Deep within the dense, untamed forest, a creature of the night prowled silently. Her fur, dark as midnight, glistened under the pale moonlight. Her eyes, a fierce and glowing amber, scanned the surroundings with a predatory intensity. She was the sister of the Dogman that Adam, Rick, and Jerry had killed a year ago, a creature driven by a powerful instinct for revenge.

The morning after her brother's death was burned into her memory. She hadn't been there when he was killed, but she had arrived too late, the scene still heavy with the scent of his killers and the unmistakable stench of his blood. The air carried the lingering traces of human sweat and fear, mingling with the metallic tang of death. She had howled in anguish and fury, vowing to avenge him.

She knew where the men responsible lived, her keen senses having tracked their scents back to their homes.

However, just as she was ready to seek her revenge, she realized something that stopped her in her tracks, she was pregnant.

Instincts honed by nature's harshest laws took over. She retreated to her den, a hidden cave deep in the forest, to ensure the safety of her unborn pups. The months passed, and she focused on her new role as a mother, nurturing and protecting her offspring. The need for revenge simmered beneath the surface, kept at bay by her maternal duties.

When the time came, and her pups were weaned and strong enough to survive without her constant presence, she left them with her extended family, other Dogmen who lived deeper within the forest. With her pups safe, the fire of vengeance rekindled within her. She resumed her hunt with a renewed sense of purpose and a deadly resolve. Her senses were sharper than ever, her instincts honed by the need to protect and avenge.

She roamed the outskirts of towns, avoiding detection, striking at unsuspecting prey to keep her strength up. Animals fell victim to her claws and teeth, but humans were her true targets.

The scent trails of Adam, Rick, and Jerry still lingered in her mind, guiding her steps. She knew where they lived, knew their habits. She could have attacked them individually, but she wanted more than just their deaths. She wanted them to feel the fear and helplessness her brother had felt. She wanted them to suffer.

As she moved closer to the town, her presence began to stir unease among wildlife. Birds fell silent as she passed, and smaller creatures scurried away, sensing the predator in their midst.

She would wait for the perfect moment. A moment when their guard was down. She would strike when they least expected it, bringing the full force of her wrath upon them. And then, she would watch as the light of life faded from their eyes, just as it had from her brother's.

As she stalked the shadows and moved from town to town, the townspeople of Butler Country went about their daily routines, blissfully unaware of the terror lurking just beyond the edge of the forest. The Dogman's hunger for retribution was a storm waiting to be unleashed, and whoever crossed her path in the meantime would pay the price for her brother's death.

The Dogman's patience was nearly at an end. Soon, she would have her revenge. The night was her ally, the darkness her cloak. She was a silent predator, driven by a fierce and unrelenting purpose. And nothing would stand in her way.

CHAPTER 1

"Can you believe we're out here at this hour?" Joe grumbled, his breath visible in the cold dawn air. He leaned on his shovel, glancing down the deserted Main Street. "All because some bigwig complained about the potholes."

Malik chuckled, adjusting his gloves. "Welcome to Carlisle, where perfection is expected before sunrise. Think we'll get overtime for this?"

Joe snorted. "Overtime? You're dreaming."

Joe was a lanky man in his early thirties, with a mop of unruly brown hair and a perpetual smirk that made him look younger than his years. He was known for his quick wit and even quicker temper, traits that often got him into trouble. Despite his complaints, he was one of the hardest workers on the crew, always ready to shoulder more than his share of the load.

Malik, on the other hand, was a stocky man in his late twenties with a full beard and a love for country music that he frequently subjected the crew to during their breaks. He had a laid-back demeanor that balanced Joe's fiery personality, and the two had formed a fast friendship since Malik joined the crew two years ago.

Frank Collins, the foreman, stood a few feet away, cigarette dangling from his lips, his face set in a permanent scowl. Frank was in his fifties, with a thick mustache and a gravelly voice that commanded respect. He had been working for the town's public works department for over two decades and had seen his fair share of midnight repairs and emergency callouts. Tonight, however, something just felt different, like the air was thicker than normal.

"Less talk, more work," he barked, the cigarette bouncing with each word. "We've got until dawn to get this done, and I don't want to hear any more whining."

The crew moved sluggishly, their shovels scraping against the asphalt as they filled the gaping potholes.

Joe and Malik exchanged glances. "What's eating him tonight?" Malik said, shoveling hot asphalt into a particularly large pothole.

"Probably the fact that he's stuck here with us fools

instead of sleeping in his warm bed," Joe replied

Frank's patience was wearing thin. "I said, get back to work!", he snapped, tossing his cigarette to the ground and grinding it under his boot.

Bill, the oldest member of the crew, was working further down the street. In his sixties, Bill had a stooped back and a slow, deliberate way of moving that belied his age. He had been with the department longer than anyone could remember, a fixture in the town, known for his kind heart and endless stories about the "good old days." Tonight, though, he seemed quieter than usual, focused on his task.

The men resumed their labor, though their movements were now tinged with a nervous energy. Frank, noticing the change, growled in frustration. "What the hell is wrong with you two?"

Before Joe could respond, a blood-curdling scream pierced the night. The crew froze, their eyes darting towards the source of the sound. It came from the far end of the street, where Bill had been working alone.

"Bill!" Frank shouted, his heart pounding as he sprinted towards the sound.

What he found stopped him in his tracks. Bill lay on the

ground, his body twisted and broken, his eyes wide open in terror. Deep gashes marred his chest and neck, blood pooling around him.

"Oh my God," Joe whispered, coming up behind Frank. What the hell happened?"

Malik stumbled backward, putting a hand over his mouth. "We need to call the Sheriff. Now."

Frank's mind raced as he looked out into the darkness. He had seen a lot in his years on the job, but nothing like this. "Run!" he shouted, his voice cracking with fear. "Get to the truck!"

As the crew hurried back, another scream echoed through the night, this time closer. Frank turned just in time to see a blur of dark fur and fangs as something lunged from the shadows, tackling Joe to the ground. Joe's scream was cut short as the creature tore into him, the sound of ripping flesh filling the air.

Malik and the remaining crew members sprinted towards the truck, their breath coming in ragged gasps. Frank followed, his eyes darting around, trying to catch a glimpse of their attacker.

As they reached the truck, Frank fumbled with the keys,

his hands shaking. He finally managed to unlock the door and shove his men inside. "Get in, get in!"

Just as he was about to climb in himself, he heard another scream. He turned to see Malik being dragged into the darkness, his fingers clawing at the pavement, leaving bloody trails. The creature's eyes glowed a menacing orange, and its snarl made Frank's stomach churn.

Frank slammed the door shut and started the engine. He didn't look back as he sped down Main Street, the truck's tires squealing on the asphalt. The few remaining crew members sat in stunned silence, their eyes wide with fear.

"What the hell was that?" one of them whispered, his voice trembling.

Frank didn't answer. He didn't know. All he knew was that something monstrous was lurking in Carlisle and had killed half of his team. As they sped towards safety, the night remained dark, the moon casting eerie shadows on the empty street behind them.

And in those shadows, the creature watched, its eyes glowing with a hunger that promised it wasn't finished yet. It was just getting started.

Frank tried to calm his breathing as he pushed the truck

to its limits. The few miles to the sheriff's office felt like an eternity, each second stretching out in agonizing fear and uncertainty. His mind replayed the horrific scenes in a loop, each detail etched into his memory with painful clarity.

When they finally screeched to a halt outside the sheriff's office, Frank wasted no time. He practically leapt out of the truck, his boots pounding the pavement as he ran inside. The remaining crew followed closely, half expecting the creature to jump out of the nearby bushes.

Deputy Reggie Harris had been with the Carlisle Sheriff's department for nearly twenty years. A stout man in his forties, Reggie was known for his neatly trimmed mustache and no-nonsense demeanor. He was the rock of the sheriff's office, always calm and collected, his steady presence a comfort to the townsfolk. His days were typically filled with routine patrols and helping lost pets find their way home, not dealing with the kind of horror that was about to unfold before him.

Reggie's shift had started like any other. He had sipped his bitter coffee, listened to the familiar murmur of the police radio, and chatted with the few night shift officers. Carlisle was always quiet in the early hours, the stillness broken only by the occasional passing car or distant bark of a dog. It was a peaceful, predictable existence, one that Reggie had come to appreciate deeply.

But the sight of Frank Collins and his disheveled crew bursting into the office shattered that morning calm. The look on their faces—ashen, eyes wide with terror—was enough to make Reggie's heart skip a beat. He hadn't seen fear like that in all his years on the force.

"Frank? What the hell's going on?" Harris asked, standing up and pushing his chair back.

Frank drew a deep breath, trying to steady his shaking hands. "We were fixing potholes on Main Street. Something attacked us. Bill, Joe, and Malik are dead. It's some kind of... creature."

Harris's eyes widened in disbelief. "A creature? Frank, are you serious?"

Emilio, who had been silent until now, stepped forward, his voice trembling. "We saw it. It was huge, covered in black fur, with glowing eyes. It killed them, Reggie. Tore them apart."

Harris ran a hand through his thinning hair, trying to process the information. "Alright, everyone calm down. Let's take this one step at a time. Start from the beginning."

Frank recounted the night's events, his voice steady despite the turmoil inside. He described the scream, the sight of Bill's mangled body, and the terrifying moments when the creature attacked Joe and Malik. Harris listened intently, his face growing more serious with each passing minute.

"Alright," Harris said finally, grabbing his radio. "10-67. I'm going to need backup on Main Street 10-17. There's been a situation. Possible dangerous animal. Proceed with caution."

He turned back to Frank and the crew. "You guys stay here. I will meet my team on Main Street to investigate. In the meantime, I need you to write down everything you remember. Every detail could be important."

Frank nodded, his hands still trembling as he took the notepad Harris handed him. The crew sat down, their minds a blur as they tried to piece together the nightmare they had just lived through.

Deputy Harris pulled Frank aside as the others wrote their statements. "Frank, you've been around here a long time. You ever seen anything like this before?"

Frank shook his head, his eyes haunted. "Never. This is something else, Reggie. It's not natural."

Harris nodded grimly. "Alright. We'll get to the bottom of this. Just hang tight."

Hours passed in a blur. The sun climbed higher, casting a harsh light on the town that now felt forever changed. Frank and the crew sat in the office, their statements completed, but the sense of dread lingered. They couldn't shake the feeling that the creature was still out there, waiting.

Eventually, Sheriff John Ryder, a tall man with a stern face and a reputation for being unflappable, entered the office. His presence commanded attention, and the room fell silent.

"Frank," Ryder said, nodding to the foreman. "I've been briefed on the situation. We've got deputies combing Main Street and the surrounding area. We'll find this thing, whatever it is."

Frank stood. "We need to make sure no one else gets hurt, Sheriff. I'll never get last night outta my head."

Ryder's eyes softened slightly. "We will. And I appreciate you and your men staying strong through this. We'll keep you updated. You are welcome to leave."

As the crew was finally allowed to leave the station, they stepped outside into the harsh daylight. The town of Carlisle seemed deceptively peaceful, the events of the night a stark contrast to the calm morning.

Frank looked at his remaining men, their faces etched

with exhaustion and fear. "Go home, get some rest. We'll be in touch."

They nodded, dispersing slowly, each man heading towards a different part of town, yet all carrying the burden of terror and loss.

Frank lingered for a moment, staring down the street towards where it all began. The shadows of the night had receded, but the memory of the creature's glowing eyes and the screams of his friends remained vivid.

CHAPTER 2

Two towns over in Hickory, the morning sun streamed through the windows of a quaint diner, casting a warm glow over the checkered tablecloths and the polished counter. Adam sat in a corner booth with his two closest friends, Jerry and Rick. Their plates were piled high with bacon, eggs, and toast, the air thick with the scent of fresh coffee and sizzling butter.

It was a rare moment of normalcy. A chance to catch up. To pretend, even for a little while, that their lives hadn't been irrevocably changed by the events of a year ago.

Jerry, a burly man with a thick beard and an easy laugh, leaned back in his seat, a forkful of scrambled eggs hovering halfway to his mouth. "So, Adam," he said, eyes twinkling with curiosity, "how's Ruby? You guys hit eleven months, right?"

Adam sighed, pushing his food around his plate. "Yeah. Eleven months." He hesitated, then exhaled through his nose. "But lately, it just feels like all we do is fight."

Rick, wiry and sharp-eyed, looked up from his coffee, his expression unreadable. "What about?"

Adam's frustration was evident as he ran a hand through his hair. "Everything. The house. My panic attacks. The nightmares. She was great about it at first, super patient. But the past few months, it's like she's tired of it. Of me." He let out a humorless laugh. "Can't really blame her. Who wants to live with someone who wakes up screaming and checks the locks five times a night?"

Jerry shook his head. "Man, I get it. Since that night, I still wake up drenched in sweat, dreaming about that thing. Sometimes I wake up and don't even know where I am for a second. It's like it never really left."

Rick nodded slowly. "Same here. That night changed everything."

A year ago, the three of them had faced something out of a nightmare. A Dogman had attacked them, killing Adam's neighbor, Dan Ludlow. They had fought back, managed to kill it, but that night had left scars, ones that weren't just physical.

For Adam, the fear had followed him. He had left his rural home for town, hoping that being surrounded by people would help. He had spent thousands securing his house. Cameras, alarms, extra locks. But none of it changed the fact that every noise in the dark sent his pulse into overdrive.

"Ruby put up with it for a long time," Adam admitted. "At first, she even helped. Would check the doors with me, remind me to breathe when I had a panic attack, console me after the nightmares. But after a while, she started getting irritated. Like it was just too much." He tapped a finger against his coffee cup. "She thinks I'm over-the-top. That I'm making us live in a damn bunker."

Jerry frowned. "You're not over-the-top, man. You're just trying to stay safe. I am sure if she had seen the damn thing she would want to live in a secure home."

Adam scoffed. "Yeah, well, tell that to Ruby. She says it's like living in a prison."

Rick studied him carefully. "You think she's checking out?"

Adam hesitated. "I don't know. Maybe. She's been distant. On her phone a lot. Going out more." His voice dropped, thick with unease. "I don't want to think it, but what if she's seeing someone else?"

Jerry set his fork down. "That doesn't sound like her, man. Have you talked to her about it?"

Adam stared at his plate. "No. I don't know how to bring it up without sounding paranoid."

Rick leaned forward, resting his elbows on the table. "You need to talk to her, Adam. If you're having doubts, you need to clear the air. Keeping it bottled up will only make things worse."

Jerry nodded. "Rick's right. You owe it to yourself and to Ruby to find out what's going on."

Adam exhaled slowly, rubbing the back of his neck. His friends were right. He couldn't keep avoiding it.

"Yeah," he said finally. "I'll talk to her tonight."

He forced a small smile. "At least I got good ole Fletcher for company."

Jerry chuckled. "That dog's probably more loyal than half the people I know."

Before Adam could respond, the bell above the diner's door jingled, drawing their attention. A familiar figure walked in.

Deputy Jesse Rodriguez.

They had gotten to know him well during the Dogman's reign of terror at Adam's cabin. He had been the first deputy on the scene, and even after everything, he had checked in on them from time to time.

Rodriguez scanned the diner until his gaze locked onto them. His usual easy-going demeanor was absent. His expression was tense, unreadable.

"Morning, gentlemen," Rodriguez greeted, tipping his hat. "Mind if I join you for a minute?"

Jerry shifted over, making room in the booth. Jesse slid in, resting his forearms on the table.

"What's up, Rodriguez?" Rick asked, already sensing something wasn't right.

Rodriguez glanced around, lowering his voice. "I thought you guys should know. There was an incident in Carlisle earlier this morning."

Adam felt a prickle of unease creep up his spine. "What kind of incident?"

Rodriguez hesitated, his fingers tapping lightly against the table. "I can't say much. But a few road workers were killed. Looks like they were attacked by an animal."

The three men exchanged tense glances.

"Oh, no," Rick said. His voice barely above a whisper. "What kind of animal?"

Rodriguez shook his head. "They don't know yet. Still investigating. But given what you guys have been through, I figured you'd want to hear about it."

Adam's stomach dropped. "You think it could be another Dogman?"

Rodriguez exhaled sharply. "I don't know, Adam. But until we find out more, you all need to stay alert."

The mood at the table became oppressively heavy.

The past year had been a fragile attempt at returning to normal. But as Rodriguez sat there, his face drawn with worry, that illusion shattered.

"Thanks for the heads-up, Rodriguez," Jerry said, his voice unusually tight.

Rodriguez nodded and stood. "Take care, guys. And if you hear or see anything unusual, you know where to find me."

They watched him leave, the bell above the door jingling again as he stepped out into the morning sun.

The silence between them stretched.

Under the table, Adam's fingers laced together as his anxiety grew. He had spent the past year trying to convince himself that night was behind them.

But deep down, he had always known the fear would find its way back.

And now, it had.

CHAPTER 3

Hickory's Sheriff Scott Walters leaned back in his worn leather chair, staring at the ringing phone on his desk. The call he had been expecting all morning was finally coming through. He took a deep breath, ran a hand through his graying hair, and picked up the receiver.

"Sheriff Walters here," he said.

"Walters, it's John," came the voice of Sheriff John Ryder from Carlisle, the neighboring town where the brutal attacks had taken place earlier that morning. John's voice was usually calm, but today it was tinged with urgency and concern.

"John, what the hell happened over there?" Walters asked, cutting straight to the point.

"It's bad, Walters," John replied. "We had a road crew come

into the station just before dawn. They were working the early shift and three of their men were killed. Torn to shreds."

Walters felt a chill run down his spine. "Torn to shreds? By what?"

"We don't know yet," John admitted. "But it looks like an animal attack. A vicious one. The coroner's initial report suggests something big, with claws. Unlikely a bear."

The sheriff closed his eyes for a moment, the memories of the Dogman incident flooding back. "Jesus, John. Do you think it could be... another one of those creatures we dealt with?"

There was a pause on the other end of the line. "I don't know. But I've got a bad feeling about this. I know you mentioned last year about that wolf creature you had problems with. But, I hope to God there isn't another bloody one."

Sheriff Walters exhaled slowly, trying to steady his nerves. "You and me both. So, what are you doing about it?"

"We've got deputies canvassing the area for any witnesses or evidence," John said. "But people are scared, Walters. Word's getting out, and with those "rumors" they've all heard from last year, I am worried people will panic."

The sheriff nodded, even though John couldn't see him.

"You're right. Keep your men on high alert. Let me know if you need me to send a couple of my deputies over to assist. We should work together on this."

"Agreed," John said. "And Walters, there's something else. The FBI has been notified. They're sending a team this afternoon. I bet if they determine it's another..." He paused, searching for the right word. "What was that wolf creature called?"

The sheriff didn't hesitate. "A Dogman."

John gave a sharp nod. "Right. Silly name isn't it? If they conclude it's another Dogman, they'll be taking over the investigation."

Walters's heart sank. The involvement of the FBI meant this was serious and potentially catastrophic. "Understood. I'll make sure we're ready for them. In the meantime, we'll do everything we can on our end."

"Thanks, Walters," John said, relief evident in his voice. "I appreciate it. We're gonna need all the help we can get."

"Hang in there, John. We'll get to the bottom of this," Walters said, trying to sound more confident than he felt.

After hanging up, the sheriff sat in silence for a moment,

processing the conversation. The memory of the Dogman attack at Adam Thomas' cabin was still fresh in his mind. The blood, the fear, the sense of helplessness. He remembered vividly the night he had to inform Dan Ludlow's wife, Vera, of her husband's tragic death. The look of devastation on her face had haunted him ever since. Adam and his buddies had managed to eventually kill the creature, but the scars it left behind, both physical and emotional, were still healing.

Of course, the public was told it was a bear attack, but that didn't stop the rumors from spreading. Whispers of something more sinister crept through town, possibly sparked by an overheard radio transmission, a stray comment at a bar, or a conversation caught in passing. Whether it was careless talk or something more, doubts had taken root, and not everyone believed the official explanation.

He picked up the phone again and dialed his Chief Deputy, Mark Turner. "Turner, I need you in my office. Now."

Turner had been enjoying a rare vacation with his family at the time of the Dogman attack. A week spent at a lakeside cabin, fishing with his wife and sons and lounging by the water, had been a welcome escape from the rigors of his daily responsibilities. The tranquil surroundings had provided a stark contrast to the chaos he returned to.

Mark had always prided himself on being reliable, the type

of officer who could be counted on in any situation. However, he also had a streak of arrogance, a belief that he was indispensable and always in control. Missing the Dogman attack had been a bitter pill to swallow. He had heard the stories but found it hard to believe that such a creature could exist.

Now, as he headed to the Sheriff's office, Mark felt the gravity of the new crisis. Concern lingered, but beneath it, a spark of excitement flickered. Small-town policing could be dull at times, and this, whatever it was, had the potential to shake things up. One of the Carlisle deputies had briefed him on the animal attacks, and while the situation was serious, it also presented a rare chance to uncover some real answers.

Within minutes, Mark stepped into the office, ready to hear why the Sheriff had called him in. "What's going on? I was in the middle of something important."

Sheriff Walters gestured for him to sit. "You've heard about the animal attack over in Carlisle right?"

Mark raised an eyebrow, his confidence unfazed. "Yeah. Are you thinking it's another one of those supposed Dogman things?"

The sheriff nodded gravely. "It's a possibility. The FBI is getting involved, and they're sending a team this afternoon. If they determine it's another Dogman, they'll be taking over the investigation."

Mark leaned back in his chair, a smirk playing on his lips. "Well, of course they are. But they're not needed. I wasn't here for the last attack, but if there is such a thing as a 'Dogman,'"— he used air quotes—" then we're better equipped now to take it out quickly."

Sheriff Walters suppressed a sigh. Mark's arrogance could be grating, but he knew the deputy's skills were valuable. "I need you to organize our deputies, increase patrols, especially near the town borders, and get the word out to the community to be on the lookout for a wild animal. People need to be cautious."

Mark nodded, already making notes. "Got it."

"Good," Sheriff Walters said, leaning forward. "Remember, we need to cooperate fully with the FBI. But we also need to do our own due diligence."

"Of course, Sheriff," Mark said, standing up. "We'll handle it. Don't worry."

As Mark left, Sheriff Walters stared at the stack of reports on his desk.

He picked up the phone one more time, dialing a number

he knew by heart. It rang a few times before a familiar voice answered.

"Adam, it's Sheriff Walters. I know Deputy Rodriguez already informed you about the attack in Carlisle this morning. We should talk."

Adam's voice was tense on the other end. "Yeah, Sheriff," I heard. What do you need?"

"We need to be prepared," the sheriff said, choosing his words carefully. "The FBI is getting involved, and they'll be in Carlisle this afternoon. If they determine it's another Dogman, they'll be taking over. I want you, Jerry, and Rick to come down to the station. Your insights could be crucial."

"We'll be there," Adam said, his voice steady despite the underlying fear.

Sheriff Walters stood up, straightened his uniform, and walked out of his office.

CHAPTER 4

Adam, Jerry, and Rick walked into the Hickory Sheriff's Department with a sense of trepidation. The air carried the familiar scent of stale coffee and old paper, a place that had seen countless meetings but never one quite like this.

The sheriff stood as they entered, his face lined with concern. "Glad you made it. Come on in," he said, greeting them with a nod before ushering them toward the meeting room.

Inside, a large table dominated the space, surrounded by worn chairs that had hosted their share of tense discussions. He motioned for them to take their seats. Chief Deputy Mark Turner stood to one side, arms crossed, his usual air of confidence feeling somewhat misplaced given the seriousness of the situation.

"Thanks for coming in, guys," the sheriff began, his voice

steady but grave. "We've got a situation in Carlisle. Three road workers were killed this morning. It looks like an animal attack, but given what happened last year, we have to consider the possibility that it's another Dogman."

The three men exchanged worried glances. Adam felt a familiar knot of anxiety tighten in his chest. He took a deep breath, trying to stay calm.

Sheriff Walters leaned forward, resting his elbows on the table. "Adam, I need to know—did you ever see another Dogman? Is there any chance there could be more out there?"

Adam shook his head slowly. "No, Sheriff. I never saw another one. But I've always feared there could be more. Logically, if there was one, it stands to reason there could be others. I've been dreading this might happen again."

Jerry nodded in agreement. "We killed one, but we didn't know if it was the only one. We just wanted to survive that night."

Rick leaned back in his chair, arms crossed, his face grim. "If there are more out there, we need to be ready. What's the plan, Sheriff?"

Walters looked at Mark, then back at the men. "The FBI is getting involved. They've likely arrived in Carlisle to investigate, and they'll take over if they determine it's another Dogman. In the meantime, we need to increase patrols, secure the town borders, and inform the community to keep their eyes open. But obviously, we can't tell them it's a Dogman."

Adam narrowed his eyes. "What do we tell them, then?"

Sheriff Walters sighed. "We'll say there's a large, aggressive animal in the area. You know the drill. It'll keep people cautious without causing panic or people not taking us seriously either."

Mark stepped forward, a smirk playing on his lips. "If there is such a thing as a Dogman, my deputies and I can handle it. We don't need the FBI throwing their weight around and getting in the way."

Adam bristled at Mark's arrogance. "Listen, Mark, there *is* such a thing as a Dogman. We faced it, and we barely survived and Dan Ludlow unfortunately didn't. Don't underestimate it."

Mark's smirk faltered slightly, but he remained defiant. "Alright, Adam. I get that it was tough, but we're more prepared this time. We'll handle it."

Sheriff Walters shot Mark a warning look, then turned back to Adam, Jerry, and Rick. "Good. Remember, we need to cooperate fully with the FBI. But we also need to do our part in ensuring the townspeople are safe."

"Don't worry, Sheriff," Mark said, standing up. "We'll handle it better than the FBI could."

Adam swallowed hard. "You'd better hope you're right, Mark. Because if you underestimate this thing, you'll be risking not only your life but the lives of your deputies and everyone in this town."

The tension in the room was evident. The sheriff intervened, his voice firm. "Alright, that's enough. We need to stay focused on the task at hand. Adam, Jerry, Rick, thank you for your insights. We'll stay in touch."

As they left the sheriff's office, Adam felt a sense of foreboding settle over him. They had faced the Dogman once before, but the stakes felt even higher now. The thought of another encounter filled him with dread, but he knew they had no choice. They had to protect their town, their loved ones, and each other.

Jerry was the first to break the silence. "So, what now? We can't just sit around and wait for the FBI to figure this out."

Adam nodded, his mind spun. "I agree. We need to prepare ourselves. We've been through this before, and we know what we're up against, even if Mark doesn't believe it."

Rick glanced around, ensuring no one was within earshot. "We need a plan. We can't just rely on the Sheriff and his Deputies. They don't understand the danger like we do."

Adam looked at his friends, seeing the same determination in their eyes that he felt. "Let's meet at my place at 5 PM. We'll discuss what we can do to protect ourselves and the town."

Jerry nodded, his face set with resolve. "Agreed. Your place at 4PM.

Rick clapped Adam on the shoulder. "We'll get through this, just like last time."

Adam felt a mix of fear and determination. "Alright. See you guys at my place. We can't let another tragedy happen."

As they parted ways, Adam felt a sense of urgency driving him.

By the time he arrived home, the afternoon sun was high in the sky, casting a bright light over the town. As soon as he opened the door, his dog Fletcher greeted him enthusiastically, tail wagging furiously. Adam knelt down, burying his face in Fletcher's fur, grateful for the dog's unconditional love and comfort.

He walked into the kitchen, trying to keep his composure, but the overwhelming stress of the situation triggered a panic attack. His breath came in short, rapid gasps, and his vision blurred.

Ruby, his partner, entered the kitchen, her expression a mix of concern and frustration. They had been fighting a lot lately, mostly because of Adam's paranoia since the last Dogman attack.

"Again?" she asked, pushing Fletcher out of the way and moving to his side.

Adam struggled to speak, his chest tightening painfully. "I… I can't breathe…"

Ruby grabbed his shoulders, trying to steady him. "You need to calm down. Breathe slowly, in and out. You need to stop being so fearful all the time."

Her words, though meant to help, cut through him. Adam finally managed to get his breathing under control, but the panic still lingered. "Ruby, there was an attack on the road crew in Carlisle this morning. Three men were killed. It might be another Dogman."

Ruby's eyes widened, but then her expression hardened. "Adam, you're losing your mind and I am over hearing about the damn Dogman! You've let that night get to you, and it's ruining our lives. I can't keep living like this."

She shook her head, tears of frustration welling up in her eyes. "Either you get a grip on this, or I'm out."

Adam watched as she turned and walked away, leaving him alone in the kitchen.

His frustration boiled over, and he followed after her. "For the thousandth time, I don't control the panic attacks. And I just came from the Sheriff's station. Hearing that another Dogman is out there, nearby, sent my nerves into overdrive. And by the way, don't ever push my dog like that again."

She didn't stop. She didn't even turn around. Instead, she reached the bedroom, stepped inside, and slammed the door in his face.

Determined to take control of the situation, Adam steeled himself for the meeting with Jerry and Rick. He couldn't let fear dictate his life any longer. As the clock approached 4PM, he waited for his friends to arrive, knowing the conversation ahead would shape their next move.

When Jerry and Rick showed up, their expressions were grim but determined. Adam led them into the kitchen and nodded toward the fridge. "Coffee or a beer?"

Rick pulled open the fridge and grabbed one. "Yeah, I think we both know the answer to that."

Jerry smirked, taking his own. "Coffee's not gonna cut it tonight."

Adam popped the cap off his beer and leaned against the counter. "Alright, here's how I see it after mulling it over in my head. First, we don't even know if it's a Dogman yet. The FBI is investigating, and until we have confirmation, there's no point in jumping to conclusions, even though it's easy to do. If it is in fact another Dogman, there's no guarantee it'll come anywhere near Hickory."

Jerry took a slow sip of his beer. "So we wait for confirmation first. Then what?"

Adam nodded. "Well, that's plan A. We wait for confirmation, stay armed, stay home after dark, watch our backs, and warn anyone we come across to do the same. No unnecessary risks." He took a swig of his beer before continuing. "I also think, if it turns out to be another Dogman, it would be smart to have family members stay somewhere safe until it is taken care of."

Rick set his bottle down and exhaled. "We've been worried about this happening ever since that night. If it turns out to be real, we handle it. But I agree, no point in panicking until we have to and family members stay safe."

Jerry nodded. "Agreed."

Adam met their eyes, feeling steadier than he had all day. "Then we stick to the plan. If it's another Dogman, we come up with plan b."

Rick gave a small, firm nod. "Works for me."

They clinked their bottles together, a quiet show of unity. There was nothing more to say. They weren't going to panic, but they weren't going to be careless either. If another Dogman was out there, they would be ready.

CHAPTER 5

The Dogman stirred within the cool, damp confines of the cave, her eyes flickering open to the dim light filtering through the entrance. Daytime was her time of rest, a period to recover from the previous night's hunt. The cave was a sanctuary, hidden deep within the dense forest, away from the prying eyes of the hairless ones. She stretched her muscular limbs, the slow ripple of power beneath thick fur a reminder of her strength. Hunger gnawed at her insides, a dull but ever-present demand that would soon need to be satisfied.

She had hunted and taken down three hairless ones. With their loud machines, they had been oblivious she was stalking them, too consumed by their work, too trusting of their surroundings to sense the danger lurking nearby. By the time they noticed her, it was too late. She had seized the opportunity to feast, exact her revenge, and instil fear. Any hairless one she crossed paths with before she reached the ones she had been tracking, fell just the same. She did not pick and choose. She did not hesitate. She took them all.

Yet their flesh never satisfied her. It was soft, thin, lacking the rich depth of a true kill. She ate them only because she had already brought them down, because waste was weakness. Even now, the hunger returned, ever calling and never truly satisfied.

Though the cave provided shelter, it was never a permanent home. She did not always rest in the same place. She moved between dens, shifting locations depending on where she roamed, never lingering too long in one spot. Her scent alone was enough to keep other predators from encroaching, a silent warning to any animal foolish enough to come too close. Nothing in the wild dared challenge her.

Nothing, except for two creatures.

The hairless ones and the Watchers.

The hairless ones were dangerous. They lacked the claws of a bear or the instincts of a wolf, but they made up for it in numbers and the strange weapons they carried. The thundersticks. She had heard them before, cracking through the trees like a violent storm, tearing through flesh and bone with unnatural force. Some of the hairless ones cowered when they sensed her presence, their bodies reeking of fear. Others hunted her kind, using fire, steel, and their loud, deadly thundersticks to drive her kin into the ground. She had grown to respect them, though never to fear them.

But the Watchers were different.

She had only encountered one up close, but she had seen others, just barely. Figures in the distance, standing as still as trees, unmoving even as the wind rattled the branches around them. She had caught glimpses of their hulking forms before they faded into the deep woods, never making a sound. But the one she had faced had been much closer.

It had been many seasons ago, deep in the heart of the forest, when she had first caught the scent. It was similar to her own, strong, wild, dominant, but different. But above all, the stench had been overpowering. For her, with senses honed sharper than any other predator in the forest, the scent had been overwhelming. Musky, thick, clinging to the air like a fog. She could smell them from miles away, making them easy to avoid.

That time, however, she had chosen not to.

Curiosity had outweighed caution, and she had followed the stench, moving carefully through the trees. Then, she saw it. A towering figure, covered in thick, long hair, moving with unnatural ease for something so large. A Watcher.

They had locked eyes for only a moment, but it had been enough.

She had felt the shift in the air, the way the forest itself seemed to pause, waiting to see what would happen. She had seen the intelligence in its dark eyes, the understanding that she was no ordinary predator. But she was not foolish enough to test her strength against it. One Watcher, she might have been able to outrun or outmatch, but they never traveled alone. If one called for help, others would come, and she knew better than to face more than she could handle.

Before the encounter could turn into something more, she had used her greatest advantage, speed. She had disappeared into the trees before the Watcher could make a move. She had not seen another since, but their scent still lingered in the deepest parts of the woods. A silent presence, neither friend nor enemy. And she always remained aware of them.

Tonight, however, there were no Watchers in her woods. No hairless ones disturbing the quiet.

There was only the hunger.

She rose and sniffed the air, her keen nose sorting through the myriad of scents carried on the wind. One, in particular, stood out. Blood. Faint, but fresh. The familiar heat of hunger ignited in her belly.

Moving silently, she slipped from the cave, her movements fluid and precise. The underbrush barely rustled as she passed, her muscular frame betraying none of her weight. She was built for the hunt, for the kill, for the silent execution of anything weaker than herself.

The scent trail led deeper into the forest, weaving through thick vegetation. As she moved, the usual chorus of the wild began to fade. Small creatures scattered, birds fell silent, and the whisper of the wind seemed to hesitate. The woods understood what lurked within them, and nature itself knew to step aside.

Eventually, the scent of blood thickened, mingling with something else, wet fur, deep breaths, the musky scent of a predator. She halted, sharp eyes narrowing as she scanned the clearing ahead.

A large male black bear hunched over the torn carcass of a deer, its powerful jaws stripping flesh from bone. The bear was massive, a formidable creature by any measure, but she felt no fear. She never had. Fear was for lesser things.

She stepped forward, emerging from the shadows with slow, calculated movement. The bear sensed her instantly, lifting its head, dark eyes locking onto the new threat. A low, warning growl rumbled from its chest. She did not flinch. She did not slow.

The bear hesitated. The growl wavered. Instinct screamed within it, primal and undeniable. This was no ordinary rival. The beast before it was something different, something wrong. The bear backed away, muscles tense, reluctant to abandon its meal but unwilling to challenge what stood before it.

With one final snort, it turned and loped into the trees, leaving the kill behind. She watched it go, cold amusement flickering in her gaze. Even the mighty bowed before her.

Stepping over the carcass, she wasted no time. Teeth sank into warm flesh, tearing chunks free with effortless ease. The rush of hot blood filled her mouth, rich and satisfying, momentarily quelling the hunger that constantly gnawed at her insides. She ate swiftly, knowing well that no kill could be savored. It would never be enough. The hunger always returned.

Once her feast was finished, she left what remained of the carcass to the scavengers. She moved with the same silence she always did, disappearing into the trees like a ghost. The cave was waiting, but not for long. She would not stay there much longer.

She did not think like an animal. She was not driven by simple instinct, not entirely. A darker purpose burned within her. A memory. A grudge. A wound that had never healed. The hairless ones who thought they had rid themselves of the wrath would soon understand their mistake.

Their time was coming. The hunt was never over.

CHAPTER 6

Jerry and Rick had just stepped onto the porch when the screech of tires shattered the quiet night. Adam followed, the cool air barely registering as apprehension coiled in his chest. Seconds later, car doors slammed shut, the abrupt noise setting his nerves on edge. He exchanged a quick glance with Jerry and Rick, who were already turning toward the commotion.

The vehicles looked out of place, sleek and government-issued, a stark contrast to the quiet street.

Four men emerged, moving with purpose. The clear leader wore a suit, his posture exuding authority, while the others were clad in dark combat gear, their movements precise and controlled. His keen gaze swept over them, assessing, calculating. Without hesitation, he strode up the steps toward them.

"Evening, gentlemen," he said, flashing a badge. "FBI. We need to confirm your identities. Which one of you is Adam Thomas?"

Adam's pulse ticked faster, but he stepped forward. "That's me."

The agent gave a nod, then looked at Jerry and Rick. "And your names?"

Jerry set his jaw. "Jerry Lawton."

Rick's gaze flicked between the men in suits. "Rick Porter."

"I'm Special Agent Johnson," the leader said, tucking his badge away. "These are Special Agents Miller, David, and Hernandez. We're here regarding the incident in Carlisle."

Adam exhaled sharply. "So it's true, then? It was a Dogman?"

Johnson didn't blink. "We're not at liberty to share details with civilians. But yes, a creature resembling a large wolf attacked the road workers."

Jerry took a step closer, eyes locked onto Johnson's. "We've dealt with one before. We know what we're up against. We want in."

Johnson's voice didn't waver. "That's precisely why we're here, Mr. Lawton. The FBI doesn't need interference."

Rick let out a dry laugh, shaking his head. "You can't honestly expect us to sit around and do nothing. This isn't some stray animal. You think you can just track it and put it down?"

Johnson's response was smooth, rehearsed. "We're well aware of the risk, Mr. Porter. That's why we're handling it. You are not equipped for this kind of threat."

Adam squared his shoulders. "We've taken steps to protect ourselves. We're not amateurs."

Johnson met his stare. "The best way you can help is by keeping your heads down and staying out of our way. We have the resources, the training, and the expertise to deal with this. You do not."

No one spoke. Jerry shifted his weight slightly, Rick's hands twitched at his sides, and Adam felt the heat rising in his chest.

Then Johnson's voice took on a more measured tone. "I get it. You've been through something most people wouldn't believe. But this isn't your fight anymore. If you interfere, you could put yourselves and others at risk."

Adam exhaled, keeping his voice even. "Fine. We'll stay out of your way. But we need to know what's happening."

Johnson gave a clipped nod. "We'll do our best to keep you updated, but this is a federal investigation. Our priority is public safety." He hesitated, then added, "Rest assured, we'll have it captured in no time."

Without another word, the agents turned and walked back to their SUVs. The visit had been swift, calculated, and left an unmistakable warning behind. Adam, Jerry, and Rick stood on the porch, watching the black vehicles speed down the road and disappear into the night.

Rick was the first to break the quiet. "They have to know what they're doing, right? The FBI doesn't just walk into something like this blind."

Adam ran a hand down his face, his thoughts a blur. "They've probably dealt with things like this before. Maybe not often, but enough to know what to expect."

Jerry shook his head. "You two really believe that? They walked in here talking like they had a damn instruction manual on how to handle this thing."

Rick frowned. "They're trained, Jerry."

Jerry let out a rough breath. "Training doesn't mean a

damn thing when you don't know what you're up against."

Adam's gut told him Jerry had a point. "I hope you're wrong," he said.

Jerry let out a short, humorless laugh. "Yeah, me too."

Rick crossed his arms. "Either way, we're not just standing around waiting for updates. We stay armed, stay home after dark, and if we run into anyone who doesn't know what's out there, we warn them. Just like we said earlier."

Adam and Jerry nodded. The FBI might be handling this, but deep down, none of them truly believed it would end that easily.

CHAPTER 7

Rick left Adam's with a heavy heart. The confirmation of another Dogman attack, and his thoughts were a storm of worry and determination. The drive home felt longer than usual, the winding country roads stretching endlessly under the overcast night sky. He couldn't help but replay the events of the past year in his mind, the fear, the bloodshed and the aftermath. They had thought it was over, but now it seemed the nightmare was continuing.

Rick lived on a sprawling farm about five miles outside of Hickory. The farm had been in his family for generations, a legacy he was proud to uphold. His wife, Macey, worked as an accountant in town, balancing the books for several local businesses. Their two children, Sascha and Renny, were both away at college, pursuing degrees that would hopefully lead them to successful futures far from the dangers that now haunted their hometown.

As he turned onto the long gravel driveway leading to the farmhouse, Rick's thoughts shifted to his wife. Macey had been his rock through the ordeal of the previous year. Her practical nature and unwavering support had helped him keep his sanity. He dreaded the conversation they would need to have, but he knew he had to tell her about the new threat.

"Hey, I am glad you're home," she said, wiping her hands on a towel. "Everything okay?"

Rick forced a smile, but he knew it didn't reach his eyes. "Hey, Mace. We need to talk."

Her smile faded, replaced by a look of concern. "What's wrong, hun?"

He took her hand and led her to the kitchen table, sitting down across from her. "It looks like there is another Dogman. The FBI confirmed the attack over in Carlisle this morning was by a Dogman."

Macey's eyes widened in shock. "Oh, no. I thought... I thought it was over."

Rick shook his head. "So did I."

Macey took a deep breath, steadying herself. "Okay. What

do we need to do?"

Rick paused, taking a moment to gather his thoughts before continuing. "Mace, I think it would be best if you went to your parents' place for a few days. Just until this passes."

Macey's eyes widened in surprise. "What? No, hun. I'm not leaving you here alone to deal with this."

"It's not about me," Rick said, his voice firm but gentle. "It's about keeping you safe. If the Dogman comes to Hickory, I don't want you anywhere near it."

Macey shook her head. "I can't just leave you here. We're a team, remember?"

Rick sighed, as he leaned closer to her. "I know, Mace. But we have to think practically. Your parents' place is safer right now. Jerry and I will be staying at Adam's place for a little while. He has fortified his place like Fort Knox."

Macey looked torn, her eyes searching Rick's face for any sign of doubt. Finally, she nodded, tears welling up in her eyes. "Okay, hun. I'll go. But you promise me you'll be extra careful."

Rick pulled her into a tight hug, feeling grateful she didn't protest too much. "I promise. As soon as it's safe, I'll let you know."

The next hour was a whirlwind of activity as Macey packed a bag and made arrangements to stay with her parents. Rick called her parents to explain the situation, ensuring they were ready to receive her. The urgency of the situation left no room for hesitation, and soon enough, Macey was ready to leave.

Rick walked her to the car, a sense of relief mixing with his anxiety. He still didn't like the idea of her driving at night, but at least she was heading in the opposite direction of Carlisle. That was the right call, even if it didn't make saying goodbye any easier.

"Take care of yourself," Macey said, her voice trembling. "And call me every day, okay?"

"I will," Rick promised, kissing her forehead. "I love you, Mace. Stay safe."

"I love you too," she replied, getting into the car. She looked at him one last time before starting the engine and pulling away.

Rick watched her car disappear down the driveway, a sense of emptiness settling over him. He knew he had made the right choice, but the farm felt lonelier without her. He released a slow measured breath, steeling himself for the days ahead.

CHAPTER 8

The Dogman rested in the darkness of the cave, her body at ease but never truly still. She had fed only hours ago, tearing into warm flesh, stripping muscle from bone until her hunger had been temporarily eased. Blood still clung to her fangs when she had curled into the safety of her den and slipped into sleep.

But sleep never lasted long.

Even in stillness, her ears twitched at the faintest shift in the wind. Her nose tested the air for anything unfamiliar. Instinct never allowed her to fully relax. The hunger never truly faded. Deep in her bones, it stirred again, urging her back into motion.

Night had settled over the land, bringing the forest to life. The Dogman rose, stretching her limbs before stepping toward the cave entrance. Cool night air filled her lungs. Her muscles moved with ease as she stepped into the shadows of the trees. The pale eye of the night was full, giving the hairless ones better sight, but not enough. They would never see her coming.

She moved soundlessly through the forest. Each step was placed with practiced precision. The air carried the usual scents. The musk of deer. Damp soil. The distant stench of something rotting. Everything was as it should be.

Then, something changed.

A shriek split the night, tearing through the stillness. The sound was unfamiliar, too loud, too sharp.

She halted, ears standing tall. She knew the sounds of the forest. She knew when something did not belong.

She lifted her head and inhaled deeply. The air carried something foreign. A thick, bitter tang that burned her nose. Something acrid clung to it, heavy and unnatural.

And beneath it, something she did recognize.

Blood.

Her muscles coiled as she shifted into motion. She moved without a sound, weaving between the trees like a wraith. The glow of flickering lights cut through the darkness, reflecting off jagged debris.

The wreck lay broken across the road, two vehicles twisted together in a mangled heap. One had flipped onto its roof, the scent of scorched metal thick in the air. The other had wrapped itself around a tree, the warm, iron-rich scent of blood leaking from within.

Something moved.

A weak cough, barely audible over the ticking of cooling metal.

The Dogman's glowing eyes narrowed. She never missed the opportunity for an easy kill.

****

Elliana had been driving to see her daughter.

She had been excited. It had been too long since she last saw her and the grandkids. The distance had never felt like much before, but lately, every mile had felt longer. She had played out the conversation in her mind, the news she would tell, the gifts she would give the little ones.

The road had been quiet. No traffic, just long stretches of dark pavement winding through the trees and pastures.

Then, headlights.

Blinding, sudden, veering into her lane.

She had sucked in a breath, yanked the wheel hard, tires screeching...

Now, pain.

It pulsed through her body in relentless waves. Each breath was shallow and labored. A coppery taste coated her tongue, thick and metallic.

The world blurred, shifting between darkness and the flickering glow of hazard lights. Smoke filled the air, searing her throat with every inhale. A deep gash above her brow sent warmth trickling down her face. She blinked hard, but her vision refused to clear.

Something was wrong.

Not just the pain. Not just the stabbing aches that made movement impossible. This was deeper. A knowing.

She was dying.

Swallowing against the rising panic, she tried to move. Agony exploded through her leg, white-hot and blinding. A strangled gasp tore from her throat.

Beyond the shattered windshield, the other vehicle lay in ruin. The driver's side door hung open, the seat empty. The passenger was gone.

The acrid smell of smoke clung to the air, but something else cut through it.

A foul, rancid stench.

Wet dog, but worse. Stronger. Sharper.

It curled in her nose, thick and nauseating. It smelled like decay, like something wild and unclean, like old blood soaked into fur.

Her stomach churned.

At first, the sound barely registered. A sharp *tap* against the pavement. Then another.

A pattern.

Her heart skipped a beat.

Coyote maybe?

She did not like the idea of anything moving so close. Injured and trapped, she had no way to keep it away. No way to fight back if something decided to investigate the wreck.

Then, another sound.

Heavier. Closer.

She thought of a bear.

It wasn't unheard of, especially near the woods. If a bear had been drawn by the scent of blood, she was in more danger than she realized. A bear could rip a door off a car with ease, could crush bones with a single swipe of its paw.

Panic clawed at her chest.

She twisted in her seat, ignoring the white-hot pain in her leg. Her hands fumbled against the seatbelt, fingers slick with blood. She tugged hard, but it held tight.

Another tap. Closer.

The unmistakable sound of nails against pavement.

Elliana froze.

A heavy *thud* landed against the hood of the car.

The entire vehicle rocked beneath the sudden weight.

A shape loomed in the fractured glow of the hazard lights. Broad shoulders. A sloped head. Eyes like fire staring through the shattered windshield.

It didn't look like a bear.

Slow, raspy breathing fogged against the cracked glass.

Maybe I'm imagining things, she thought.

It moved, pressing one clawed hand against the windshield.

A delicate cracking sound whispered through the silence.

It was testing it.

Elliana's lips moved without sound, whispering prayers that barely formed in her mind.

Please God. Make it go away.

Her voice was hoarse, barely audible, repeating in a desperate loop.

The crack beneath its claws spread outward.

Then...

Lights.

Bright white beams cut through the darkness from behind. Headlights.

Elliana's breath hitched.

Someone was coming.

Relief surged through her, a desperate, fleeting hope that

help had arrived. If they saw the wreckage, they would stop. They would call for help and whatever the creature was would run away.

She turned her head toward the approaching glow...

The windshield shattered.

Glass rained down on her as something massive crashed through the opening. A scream tore from her throat, the sound drowned by the blast of hot, reeking breath as the Dogman lunged forward.

She barely had time to react before claws tore through the seatbelt.

Fangs sank deep into her shoulder.

Pain exploded through her body.

A world of even more pain.

Then, blackness.

CHAPTER 9

Darren Holt drummed his fingers against the steering wheel, nodding along to Slipknot blasting from the speakers. The sun had just set, leaving the sky cast in deep blue. His headlights cut through the dimming light as he followed the winding stretch of Old Mill Road.

He checked the clock on the dash. 6:34 PM.

Late.

His girlfriend was going to be pissed. He'd promised to be in Hickory by six, but work ran long, and he had lost track of time. A couple of text notifications already showed on his center display.

Up ahead, hazard lights pulsed weakly, flickering against the trees.

His foot eased off the gas as he approached the wreckage.

Two cars. One crumpled in the middle of the road, its front end smashed in, the other flipped onto its roof farther down, wheels still faintly spinning.

The accident must have just happened.

Darren scanned the wreck, expecting to see someone moving, stumbling out, waving him down for help.

No one.

His fingers hovered over his phone. Should he call 911?

As his car crept past the first vehicle, something sprawled across the hood came into view, half inside the shattered windshield.

He gasped.

A massive, fur-covered shape hunched over the crumpled remains of the car, its lower body still outside, clawed feet dug deep into the metal. The thing was hunched low, powerful limbs shifting as it moved inside the wreckage.

A creeping dread slithered up Darren's spine.

The headlights illuminated the shape fully, bristling fur, shifting muscle, and something sickeningly human about its proportions.

The engine idled, low and steady, but his pulse pounded in his ears, drowning everything out.

A slow, calculated pullback revealed more of its face.

Amber eyes flickered in the dim light, its head shaped like a weird mix between a German Shepherd and a hyena.

He recoiled at the sight.

The thing wasn't trapped. It was feeding.

A wet, sickening crunch filled the space between them.

His stomach turned.

A mangled arm hung limply from the dashboard, torn open at the forearm.

Heat crawled up the back of his neck. His body screamed at him to floor it, but he couldn't tear his eyes away.

The creature twitched.

Darren's heart nearly burst from his chest.

His foot slammed the gas pedal.

The tires screeched against the pavement as the car

lunged forward, the engine roaring to life.

His vision blurred as he sped past the wreckage, his pulse hammering.

Something shifted in his peripheral vision.

Not chasing.

Turning.

The creature watched him leave.

Darren's breath came in desperate gasps, panic threatening to overtake him.

He was going too fast.

The road blurred past, the edges of the trees blending into dark streaks. His car veered over the center line, swaying into the wrong lane.

For a second, he thought he was about to lose control.

His arms trembled as he yanked the wheel, swerving hard, forcing himself back onto his side of the road. His tires skidded, the car fishtailing slightly before he regained control.

The wreck was gone behind him, swallowed by distance.

But the image burned into his brain.

That thing.

The way it moved.

The sound of tearing flesh.

His stomach twisted painfully as he wiped a trembling hand across his mouth.

He glanced at the center display, his stomach sinking as the signal bars sat at zero. No service.

"Come on, come on," he yelled.

The signal bars flickered, two, then three.

He immediately pressed the call button on the steering wheel. "Dial 911."

The line rang.

A voice crackled through. "911, what's your emergency?"

Darren's mouth opened, but the words stuck in his throat.

How the hell was he supposed to explain this?

He swallowed hard, forcing himself to focus.

"There's been a wreck," he finally managed, his voice hoarse. "Two cars. Old Mill Road. I think people are hurt."

His mind flashed back to the windshield.

To the thing inside it.

The blood dripping from its maw.

"Sir, did you witness the crash?"

"No," Darren whispered. "I... I was just driving through. I saw it after."

Another pause.

"Alright, we're sending emergency services now. Stay on the line. Can you give me a mile marker?"

Darren's eyes darted ahead, scanning the roadside. The next marker loomed in his headlights, barely visible in the dark.

"Yeah," he said quickly. "Mile marker eighteen. Just past it."

"Got it. Help is on the way. Stay with me."

Darren wet his lips, his grip tightening around the phone.

"Just hurry."

CHAPTER 10

Adam sipped his now-cold coffee, his eyes on the police scanner as the latest dispatch update crackled through. His phone buzzed against the table, the vibration rattling the wood.

He grabbed it and answered without hesitation.

"Hey, bud. What's up?"

"You hear those sirens?" Jerry's voice carried a note of concern.

"Yeah. Just checked the scanner," Adam said, flicking his gaze back to the device. "Car accident on Old Mill Road. Deputies and emergency responders are already on the scene."

Jerry exhaled. "Damn. That's terrible. Any word on injuries?"

Adam rubbed his jaw. "Not yet."

A pause, then Jerry asked, "How's Ruby?"

Adam leaned back in his chair. "She went out to see a few friends, apparently."

Jerry made a low sound. "Ok."

Adam didn't respond as he drummed his fingers against the table.

"Alright, man. Just figured I'd check in. Talk later."

Adam hung up, setting his phone down just as another update crackled through the scanner. Sheriff Walters and Hickory's county coroner, Dr. Victoria Portell, had arrived on the scene.

By the time Sheriff Walters pulled up to the crash, deputies and emergency responders were already working the site. The accident had drawn out a full response, fire trucks, ambulances, and police cruisers, their lights casting red and blue flashes across the dark pavement.

Two cars had collided violently. One sat overturned with the driver's door open, while the other rested in the middle of the road, its front end crumpled and windshield shattered.

Deputy Jesse Rodriguez approached as the sheriff stepped

out of his cruiser. His face was set, his usual easy-going demeanor absent.

"Bad one," Rodriguez said. "First responders got here a few minutes ago. Driver in the overturned car was ejected on impact. We found him in the ditch. I'd say he died on impact."

Sheriff Walters exhaled, his eyes scanning the wreck. "And the other driver?"

Rodriguez raised his brow. "Still in the car."

Walters turned to see Dr. Victoria Portell standing near the crushed vehicle, arms crossed. The coroner had a grim look on her face as she waved the sheriff over.

"You're going to want to see this," Purtell said.

Sheriff Walters walked toward the wreckage, ducking under the police tape. The driver's door had been nearly torn away in the crash, and the frame was twisted in a way that made it obvious there was no chance of survival.

Inside, the driver, a woman, was slumped in her seat, her head tilted at an unnatural angle. But it wasn't the impact that had killed her.

Her chest and throat had been ripped open.

Muscle and sinew were torn apart, blood soaking through

what remained of her clothing. The wounds were deep and jagged.

Walters barely stopped himself from swearing.

Portell let out a slow breath. "This wasn't the accident."

Rodriguez shifted uncomfortably beside them. "An animal?"

Portell nodded. "The tearing of her throat, yeah."

Walters' stomach knotted. He had seen fatal wrecks before. He had seen deer crashes, cases where wild animals had turned up near the scene, sometimes scavenging bodies. But this wasn't scavenging.

This was an attack.

Walters turned to Rodriguez. "Where's the other body?"

"About fifty feet from his car, down in the ditch," Rodriguez said as he pointed.

"No signs of trauma from an animal," Purtell said.

Sheriff Walters took in the two wrecked vehicles, the bloody seat, the way the woman had been ripped apart but left in place.

His gaze drifted toward the treeline beyond the accident. Night had fully settled now, the woods dark and silent.

A slow exhale left him.

Rodriguez spoke first. "Are you thinking what I'm thinking Sheriff?"

Walters didn't respond. He didn't need to.

CHAPTER 11

Chris Lockheart trudged home after a long shift at the warehouse, exhaustion weighing on him like a lead vest. The streetlights cast a faint glow over the empty sidewalks as he noticed the lack of people out tonight. He pulled his jacket tighter against the cool night air and adjusted his worn cap, already thinking about the dinner waiting for him at home.

As he turned onto Keefe Street, a prickle of unease crawled up the back of his neck. The street was too quiet. Normally, he'd hear the murmur of televisions through open windows, the occasional distant laughter of neighbors chatting on their porches. Tonight, there was nothing.

Chris shook his head, blaming fatigue. He kept walking, his footsteps echoing too loudly against the pavement.

Halfway down the block, he glanced up and froze.

At the far end of the street, standing beneath the dim glow of a streetlamp, was a hulking figure.

The shape was massive, unnaturally tall, its body covered in thick, dark fur that seemed to swallow the light. Glowing amber eyes burned through the darkness, locking onto him with a piercing, predatory gaze.

Chris couldn't process what he was seeing. It looked like a werewolf. His mind flashed to the rumors that had haunted the town for the past year, whispers of something unnatural lurking just beyond sight.

His heart hammered in his chest. A cold sweat broke out along his spine.

Then, the thing moved.

Chris turned and bolted.

Panic surged through him, his breath coming in short, frantic gasps as he sprinted down the street. He dared not look back, but the sound of pounding footsteps behind him told him everything he needed to know. He was being hunted.

A deep growl sent ice through his veins. It was gaining on him.

Chris pushed himself harder, his legs burning, lungs

screaming for air. The rhythmic thudding of its pursuit was deafening now, too close, too fast.

Then pain.

Claws raked across his back, shredding through fabric, grazing skin. He stumbled, nearly falling, but adrenaline kept him upright. He gritted his teeth against the pain and kept running, lungs heaving.

A sudden burst of light.

Headlights flared to life down the street, flooding the pavement.

The creature veered off, disappearing into the darkness as the car engine revved.

Chris didn't stop to question why. He took the chance and ran harder.

Up ahead, an alleyway. He made a sharp turn, feet pounding against the pavement as he darted into the narrow space. He needed cover.

A dumpster loomed near the end of the alley, half-hidden in shadow. Without thinking, he dove behind it, pressing himself against the cold, grimy metal.

He held his breath, every nerve on edge.

Heavy footsteps slowed at the alley entrance. A low growl rumbled through the air, vibrating against the brick walls. The creature was just feet away.

Chris clenched his fists, biting down on the instinct to run. He dared a glance around the edge of the dumpster.

The creature was sniffing the air, glowing eyes scanning the alley.

Chris pulled back quickly, heart slamming against his ribs. It was hunting him.

The seconds dragged on, stretching into eternity as he waited. The raspy breathing filled the alley, sniffing, searching.

Then silence.

Chris strained to listen, but all he heard was the pounding in his own head.

Had it left?

He didn't move. He barely breathed.

Minutes passed.

Then, finally, retreating footsteps. Slow at first, then fading entirely into the night.

Chris stayed frozen, unwilling to believe he was safe until the alley was empty again.

Cautiously, he peeked out. The creature was gone. The street beyond lay still.

Summoning the last of his nerve, he crept out from behind the dumpster and started moving. Fast. Keeping to the shadows, he avoided the main roads, barely registering the burning ache in his back where the claws had slashed him.

He just needed to get home.

The sight of his house brought a rush of relief. He fumbled for his keys, hands shaking, and jammed them into the lock.

The door swung open, and he slipped inside, slamming it shut behind him.

Chris leaned against the door, chest heaving, the solid barrier between him and whatever was outside the only thing keeping him together.

Then, his stomach turned violently. A wave of nausea overtook him, and he dropped to his knees, vomiting onto the entryway rug.

"Chris?"

His wife's voice jolted him. Footsteps approached fast, and

suddenly she was beside him, crouching down, her face a mask of worry.

"What's wrong?" she asked, reaching out to steady him.

Chris wiped his mouth with the back of his hand, head spinning.

Yeah, he thought wryly. I'll just tell her the truth. A werewolf chased me home. That'll go over well.

CHAPTER 12

Megan and Ellis Parker drove down the quiet, winding streets of Hickory, in an almost awkward silence. Ellis gripped the steering wheel with a mix of reluctance and resignation, his face lined with the years of enduring his mother's overbearing nature.

"I know you're not thrilled about going to my mom's place," Ellis said, his tone a mix of apology and irritation.

Megan sighed, her patience wearing thin. "It's not that, Ellis. It's just that every dinner turns into a lecture about how we should have kids by now."

Ellis rolled his eyes, his irritation growing. "Yeah, I know. It's just one night, and we promised we'd come."

As they rounded a corner onto Whittaker Street, Megan's

attention was drawn to a fleeting shadow darting out of the headlights' beam. She squinted, trying to make out what she had just seen, her heart skipping a beat.

"Ellis, slow down," she said, her voice tense.

Ellis glanced at her, confused. "What's wrong?"

"Did you see that?" Megan asked, pointing towards the spot where the shadow had disappeared. "There was something there, just now."

Ellis followed her gaze but saw nothing out of the ordinary. He frowned, squinting into the darkness. "It's probably just a stray dog or something."

Megan shook her head, her eyes wide with fear. "No, Ellis. That wasn't a dog. It looked like… it looked like a Werewolf."

Ellis laughed, a short, incredulous bark. "A Werewolf? Really, Meg? I have heard plenty of excuses before to get out of seeing my mom but this one has to take the cake!"

Megan shot her husband a stern look. "I'm serious, Ellis. It was huge and it moved incredibly fast. We need to call the Sheriff."

Ellis rolled his eyes, his frustration growing. "Come on, Meg. We're almost there. Besides, there's no such thing as

Werewolves. The Sheriff would never let me live it down if I called and said you'd seen one," he said, laughing.

As they drove past the spot where Megan had seen the shadow, she kept her eyes glued to the window, watching for any sign of movement. But the creature was gone, vanished into the night.

Ellis glanced at her, his expression softening slightly. "Look, don't worry. Whatever it was has run off now. It was probably just a bear or a big dog."

Megan shook her head, her voice trembling. "Ellis, that was not a bear. I know what I saw."

Ellis sighed, knowing he wasn't helping the situation. "Okay, okay. Let's just get to my mom's place, and we can talk about it later. Maybe it was just a trick of the light."

Megan slumped back in her seat, her fear slowly giving way to frustration. She knew what she had seen, and no amount of rationalizing from Ellis would change her mind. "Fine, but don't say I didn't warn you."

They arrived at Ellis's mother's house a few minutes later, the warm glow of the porch light a stark contrast to the chilling darkness they had just left behind. Megan stepped out of the car, her mind still trying to accept what she had seen.

Ellis joined her, placing a reassuring hand on her shoulder. "Let's just get through dinner, okay?"

Megan nodded, but the fear remained in the back of her mind. As they walked up the steps to his mother's house, she couldn't help but glance back one last time, half-expecting to see glowing eyes watching them from the shadows.

Inside, the familiar scent of home-cooked food filled the air, offering some comfort. His mother's grating voice and endless judgment quickly became more frustrating than the lingering thoughts of the creature she had seen.

CHAPTER 13

The Dogman prowled through the narrow gaps between the buildings, moving with the silent confidence of an apex predator. She had lost the scent of the human she had been chasing, the male who had barely slipped from her grasp. Frustration simmered inside her, edged with hunger, pushing her forward.

The scent of sweat and stale tobacco drifted past her, mixed with something bitter. She recognized it now, a strange, pungent smell she had come to associate with the hairless ones who dulled their senses with foul-smelling plants.

She followed the scent, her steps light and calculated, closing the distance with every breath. The sound of something rolling against the pavement reached her ears. A hairless one was approaching, unaware a predator was there.

Bobby, twenty-five and unforgivingly reckless, pedaled lazily toward the gas station, his mind sluggish. He had smoked earlier, and now the craving for something salty and sweet gnawed at him. Music pounded in his ears through his headphones, Post Malone's voice drowning out everything else as he turned onto another street, distracted and unfocused.

A flash of light came from the side as a car swerved, brakes screeching as the driver slammed to a stop. Bobby wrenched the handlebars, nearly toppling over.

"Watch it, jackass! I could have died!" he shouted, flipping the driver off as he steadied himself. His heart pounded from the near miss, but instead of relief, he felt a rush of irritation.

The Dogman had already begun stalking him, weaving between the buildings as he rode past. He was alone. Distracted. Oblivious.

She crept closer.

Bobby, unaware, fumbled in his pocket for his lighter, trying to relight the joint hanging from his lips.

The air shifted behind him.

A blur of movement struck without warning, slamming into him with enough force to send him flying off his bike. He crashed onto the pavement, his headphones clattering against the ground as his music cut off.

"What the hell?" he gasped, dazed.

Before he could react, something heavy pressed down on him. Claws bit into his back, pinning him in place. Hot breath rolled over his face, thick with the scent of raw meat.

Bobby's chest heaved as he looked up.

Glowing amber eyes burned into his as a deep snarl vibrated through his ribs.

His body jerked instinctively, muscles twisting as he fought to break free. His fingers groped along the pavement, grabbing a loose rock near the curb. He swung wildly, striking something solid.

The Dogman recoiled slightly, shaking off the hit.

Bobby scrambled onto his hands and knees, dragging himself toward his bike. Pain flared through his scraped skin, but the need to escape drowned it out.

A crushing grip clamped around his ankle.

He screamed as his leg was yanked backward, slamming him onto his stomach. Kicking wildly, his heel struck the creature's muzzle, but it barely registered.

The Dogman's jaws clamped down on his calf.

The pressure was unbearable. Teeth tore through muscle with ease. A sickening pop filled his ears as something inside his leg gave way.

Bobby howled, thrashing violently, but his movements were slowing. His energy was bleeding out of him just as quickly as the warmth pooling beneath him.

His screams grew weaker. His breath, short and ragged.

The Dogman leaned in, the scent of his fear thick in her nostrils.

Bobby's lips parted, trying to whisper something. A plea, a prayer.

Her jaws snapped shut.

His body sagged.

The Dogman lifted her head, ears flicking as she listened for movement. The night remained still.

She gripped Bobby's lifeless form and dragged him into the bushes, his blood leaving a dark smear on the pavement.

****

Margaret Dawson sighed as she reached for the remote, pausing *Judge Judy* with an annoyed click. A sharp scream had cut through the night, loud enough to break her focus.

She sat still for a moment, listening. Probably some idiot drunk or those neighborhood hooligans making a racket again. Still, she heaved herself up from the couch and shuffled to the window, pulling back the curtain just enough to peek outside.

The street was dark and quiet. No movement, no figures loitering where they shouldn't be. Just the usual porch lights glowing along the row of houses.

Margaret scoffed and let the curtain fall back into place. "Damn fools," she said as she returned to her chair, picking up the remote again. *Judge Judy* returned, her sharp voice silencing the courtroom's chaos.

Margaret settled in, pushing the noise from her mind. If whoever it was had any sense, they'd keep moving.

CHAPTER 14

Willie Remic wasn't your typical thief. He had a family, four kids with another on the way, and a wife who had long since lost patience with his endless excuses. It wasn't that Willie didn't want to work, he told himself, but no job paid enough to cover their mounting bills. Rent was late again, and his wife had been on him for days, frustration and worry clear in her voice.

He had tried odd jobs, but nothing stuck. A stint at the local gas station barely made a dent in their expenses. The pressure was suffocating, and Willie had turned to an easier solution, stealing. It was fast money, and he justified it by telling himself he was doing it for his family.

Tonight's target was already picked out, a catalytic converter from a 2023 Ford F-150 he had been eyeing for weeks. He knew a guy in Livingston who paid well and didn't ask questions. It was risky, but desperation didn't leave room for hesitation.

Willie spent the day keeping a low profile, staying out of sight. His wife, Lisa, had long since stopped asking where he disappeared to. With four kids to manage, she had enough to deal with. The less she knew, the better.

As night settled over Hickory, Willie checked his tools, a hacksaw, a wrench, and a flashlight. He dressed in dark clothes and waited until the kids were asleep and Lisa had gone to bed before slipping out the back door.

The streets were quiet, most of the town locked inside for the night. Willie moved quickly, keeping to alleys and side roads. He knew the layout better than most, which made his work easier.

When he reached the street where the F-150 was parked, his pulse quickened. He took a deep breath, steadying his nerves. He had done this before, but the fear of getting caught never faded.

The truck sat in the driveway of a well-kept house. Willie had watched the place enough to know the owner went to bed early. He crept closer, checking for movement. The street was empty, the only sound a distant car passing through town.

Sliding under the truck, he adjusted his flashlight. The catalytic converter was right where it should be. He pulled out his tools and got to work, the hacksaw biting into the metal in a steady rhythm.

As he worked, his thoughts drifted to the money he would make. It wouldn't fix everything, but it would buy them time. Maybe he could even get Lisa something nice, an apology for the stress he put her through.

The sound of approaching footsteps made him catch his breath. Slow. Heavy.

Willie froze, heart pounding. He held still, gripping the hacksaw tightly.

Someone was there. Watching.

CHAPTER 15

Doug leaned back in his worn recliner, the flickering light from the television casting shifting patterns across the room. A half-empty beer rested on the side table, condensation pooling around its base. His eyes were unfocused as he watched the game, his thoughts drifting to his pride and joy parked outside—his 2023 Ford F-150.

After a bitter divorce that left him with little more than his truck and a cheap rental, Doug had scraped together every extra dollar to buy that vehicle. It was more than just transportation; it was proof that he could rebuild, that he wasn't broken. He took pride in keeping it spotless, making sure it remained in pristine condition.

He took another sip of beer when a faint noise outside caught his attention. Metal against metal. His brow pulled together as he set the can down and pushed himself up from the recliner. The house creaked beneath his weight as he moved toward the door.

Outside, the Dogman prowled through the darkness, eyes scanning for movement. Her senses locked onto the faint shuffling ahead. A hairless one was underneath a vehicle, unaware of what was closing in.

Willie Remic had no time to react.

The creature closed the distance in a heartbeat, her powerful limbs propelling her forward. She grabbed Willie's leg and yanked him violently from beneath the truck, the sudden force wrenching it from its socket with a sickening pop. His mouth opened in a strangled gasp, but before a scream could form, she lunged for his face. Teeth sank deep, crushing bone and silencing him instantly. Blood pooled beneath him as she tore downward, her jaws working their way to his throat, ensuring there was no chance of survival.

Doug stepped onto the patio just in time to witness the carnage.

The world around him slowed. He gasped, eyes fixed on the monstrous figure looming over the lifeless body next to his truck. The glow of the creature's amber eyes locked onto his, holding him in place like a predator studying cornered prey.

Instinct finally broke through the shock, and Doug stumbled backward. The creature snarled, head tilting as if deciding whether to pursue. Doug didn't wait to find out. He turned and bolted inside, slamming the door behind him and locking it with trembling hands.

His heart pounded so hard he thought it might burst. His breath came fast. He had never known fear like this.

A crash echoed from outside.

Doug ran for the basement door, throwing it open and nearly tripping down the steps in his rush. He fumbled for his phone, his fingers so unsteady he almost dropped it.

"911, what's your emergency?"

"There's... there's a freakin' huge wolf outside," Doug stammered, his voice cracking. "It just attacked someone in my driveway. 141 Darlington. You need to send help now, please!"

"Stay inside, sir. Lock all your doors and windows. Help is on the way."

A window shattered upstairs.

Doug's blood ran cold. Heavy footsteps thudded against the floor above him, methodical, searching.

She was inside.

The noise above sent dust floating down from the ceiling. Furniture scraped across the floor. Drawers were ripped open, their contents tossed aside. She was looking for him.

Doug gripped a metal pipe from a pile of old tools, pressing himself against the far wall. He barely breathed.

Then, sirens in the distance.

The destruction upstairs came to an abrupt stop. A deep, frustrated growl vibrated through the house, followed by a loud crash as the back door was torn open.

Doug remained frozen as he waited for help to arrive.

Minutes later, Deputy Mike Davis and Rebecca Cantrell entered, their hands on their holsters as they scanned the wreckage. Doug barely registered their voices as they called out. His mind was still trying to process what had happened.

He forced himself up the stairs, gripping the railing to steady his shaking legs. The moment he stepped into the ruined living room, Deputy Cantrell turned toward him.

"Sir, are you alright?"

Doug swallowed hard. "I… I think so. It's gone. It ran when it heard the sirens."

Cantrell nodded. "We'll have deputies search the area, but

for now, let's get you checked out."

Doug stepped onto the porch, the cool night air biting against his sweat-soaked skin. His gaze drifted to his truck, covered in blood. The body beneath it was barely recognizable.

CHAPTER 16

Adam woke with a start, the sound of sirens cutting through the stillness of the night. His heart pounded as he sat up in bed, his mind struggling to shake off the remnants of sleep. Almost immediately, Fletcher came to his side, sensing his owner's distress. Patting him, Adam glanced sideways, noticing Ruby's absence. A sense of dread settled over him as he rubbed his eyes and got out of bed, with Fletcher close behind.

He moved quietly, padding down the hallway and peeking into the other rooms to make sure everything was as it should be. When he reached the top of the stairs, he saw a dim light glowing from the living room below. He descended the stairs slowly, each step filled with a growing sense of dread.

As he reached the bottom of the stairs, he saw Ruby on the

couch, her face illuminated by the soft glow of the television. She must have gotten home and decided not to come to bed. A blanket was draped over her, rising and falling with each steady breath. Adam felt a pang of guilt; their arguments had pushed her to find comfort here instead. He sighed quietly, not wanting to wake her, and made his way to check the scanner.

In his study, Adam waited for Fletcher before shutting the door and settling at his desk.

He reached for the small radio he kept there, tuned to the sheriff's channel. He had gotten into the habit of listening in, wanting to stay informed about any potential dangers, especially after the events last year.

As he adjusted the volume, the crackling static gave way to the clear voices of dispatch and deputies communicating in urgent tones.

"All units, be advised. We have a large, dangerous animal on the loose. Proceed with caution."

Adam's blood ran cold. Another attack? His mind immediately flashed back to the Dogman. The fear, the blood, the sheer terror of that night resurfaced with a vengeance.

He leaned in closer, straining to hear every word.

"Dispatch, this is Unit 7. We've secured the area. We've got one victim deceased and another in shock. The creature has fled the scene. Requesting EMT and the Coroner."

Adam's hands trembled as he switched off the radio.

Determined not to be caught off guard again, Adam immediately went to check all the windows and doors, ensuring that each one was locked and secure. He double-checked his security system, making sure all the cameras were functioning and the alarms were set. The familiar ritual calmed him slightly, but the underlying fear remained.

Just as he finished his rounds, his cell phone buzzed.

The screen lit up with Jerry's name. Adam answered quickly.

"Jerry, did you hear the sirens too?" Adam asked, his voice tense.

"Yeah, woke me up. What the hell is going on?" Jerry replied, his voice equally anxious.

"I just listened to the sheriff's channel. They reported a creature attack at 141 Darlington. A man was killed, Jerry. It's just like we feared."

There was a brief silence on the other end before Jerry

spoke again, his tone grim. "You know. I refuse to believe that this is just a coincidence that there is another Dogman so close to us."

"I know," Adam said, glancing out the window into the dark night.

Jerry agreed. "I'll call Rick and let him know."

"Alright. Talk later," Adam said.

After ending the call, Adam stood in the quiet of his study, as he rubbed the knot in his neck. He knew that this time, they had to be ready.

Adam walked back downstairs, glancing at Ruby still asleep on the couch. He didn't want to wake her, but he knew he would have to tell her everything in the morning.

CHAPTER 17

Rick's phone rang, jolting him awake. He sat up abruptly on the couch, *The Office* reruns still playing on the TV. His pulse quickened as he grabbed the phone, a sinking feeling settling in his gut. Calls at this hour were never good news.

"Hello?" Rick said as he cleared his throat.

"Rick, it's Jerry," came the urgent voice on the other end of the line. "There's been another attack. This time, it was in town."

Rick's heart sank. "What? Where in town?"

"Darlington Street. Someone's dead," Jerry replied, his voice hollow with grief and shock.

Rick closed his eyes, trying to steady himself. "Damn it. This thing is just getting started isn't it?"

"Seems so," Jerry replied.

"Macey went to her parent's place earlier. I feel better if I don't have to worry if she is safe or not."

"Good," Jerry said, relieved. "I'm going to get the boys to stay with their mom for a little while.

"Makes sense," Rick replied, running a hand through his hair. "I think we should meet with Adam tomorrow. We need to figure out what to do next."

Jerry's voice was firm but kind. "Stay sharp, Rick. We can't let our guard down, not for a second."

"I won't," Rick promised.

Rick hung up the phone and leaned against the kitchen counter, as he processed the news. He glanced at the clock on the wall; it was nearly 1 a.m. The first light of dawn was still over five hours away, and the darkness outside felt more oppressive than ever.

Rick walked back into the living room and sat down heavily on the couch. The television droned on, but he wasn't really paying attention.

He thought about Macey, safe at her parents' place for now. The decision to send her away had been difficult, but he knew it was the right one. She was his rock, and he couldn't bear the thought of something happening to her. But the separation was hard, and the house felt emptier without her presence.

Rick picked up the remote and turned off the TV. He sat in the dark for a long time, listening to the creaks and groans of the old farmhouse. Every noise made his heart skip a beat, but he forced himself to remain calm.

He got up and went to the window, peering out into the night. The farm was shrouded in darkness, the fields stretching out into the distance. He could just make out the silhouette of the barn, a dark shape against the inky sky. He watched for any signs of movement, any indication that the Dogman was near.

But the night remained still and quiet, the only sounds the distant calls of nocturnal animals. Rick turned away from the window and began to pace the room, trying to shake the anxiety that had settled over him.

CHAPTER 18

Adam was in the kitchen, pouring himself a drink when a movement caught his eye. He turned and saw Ruby sitting up, her eyes fixed on him.

"Adam, what the hell are you doing?" Ruby snapped, her voice sharp and filled with irritation. "I had just fallen asleep and you woke me up with all that noise."

"I'm sorry," Adam said, trying to keep his voice calm. "I had to check the windows and doors. I heard something on the sheriff's channel..."

Ruby cut him off, waving her hand dismissively. "I don't want to hear about your paranoia again. You're always checking and rechecking everything. It's driving me crazy!"

Adam took a deep breath, trying to keep his frustration

in check. "This isn't paranoia, Ruby. There's been another attack. A creature killed a man on Darlington Street just an hour ago. I think it's another Dogman."

Ruby rolled her eyes, clearly unimpressed. "Seriously, Adam? Another Dogman? Do you even hear yourself? You've been obsessed with this ever since that night. It's all you talk about."

Adam clenched his fists, struggling to keep his composure. "I know it sounds crazy, but it's real. We barely survived last time, and now it's back. You need to take this seriously."

Ruby stood up, crossing her arms over her chest. "I can't keep living like this, Adam. Your fear is taking over our lives. You need to get help or figure something out because I can't do this anymore."

Adam stared at her, trying to process the impact of what she was saying. He wanted to make her understand, to make her see the danger they were in, but he could see the wall she had built between them. She wasn't listening, and she didn't believe him.

"Actually," Ruby continued, her voice breaking slightly. "I'm moving out."

Adam was shocked, his eyes widening. "What? Ruby, where are you going to go?"

Ruby's expression faltered, her eyes widening slightly in shock at the mention of Eddie's name. "Yes," she said, recovering quickly, her tone turning defiant.

Adam's stomach churned. "Are you having an affair with him?" he asked, his voice barely above a whisper.

Ruby looked him straight in the eyes, her expression unyielding. "What do you expect?" she said coldly. "You don't show me enough attention. You're always worrying about safety and this Dogman nonsense. You don't even want to go out after dark. Your constant anxiety makes me feel like you're weak and that you actually *couldn't* take care of me."

Adam felt a wave of devastation wash over him. "You think I am weak?" he retorted, his voice rising. "How could you? I killed a freakin' Dogman, and you call me weak?"

Ruby's eyes flashed with anger. "Killing that creature doesn't change the fact that you're constantly on edge. I need someone who can live life with me, not just hide from it! I need someone I can be proud of. People whisper behind your back, you know."

Adam's frustration boiled over. "I'm trying to protect us!

There is another one out there, and you're acting like it's just some fairy tale."

"Protect us?" Ruby scoffed. "Or protect yourself? You live in fear, Adam. And that fear is suffocating me."

Adam took a deep breath, struggling to contain his emotions. "Fear? You think I wanted this? You think I enjoy living like this? I'm doing everything I can to keep us safe, to make sure we don't end up like those other people. I take care of everything! The bills, the chores, everything! And this is what you think of me?"

Ruby's face hardened. "It's not enough. You're not enough. I need more than just someone who pays the bills and does the chores. I need someone who can be present, who can live without constantly looking over their shoulder."

Adam's voice shook with disbelief. "Who are you, Ruby? I never knew you felt this way. I never knew you thought like this."

Ruby shook her head, her voice dropping to a bitter whisper. "It's been coming for a while now, Adam. I'm done."

With that, Ruby turned and headed upstairs to pack her things. Adam watched her go, his heart breaking with every step she took. He felt helpless, torn between the need to protect her and the realization that she may not be who he thought she was.

He sank onto the couch, burying his face in his hands. The night had taken everything from him. His peace, his security, and now, the woman he loved.

CHAPTER 19

Ruby descended the stairs slowly, her suitcase bumping against each step. The house was quiet, the weight of unspoken words lingering in the air. She paused at the bottom, her gaze sweeping over the living room, the place where laughter had once filled the space, where love had lived before it unraveled. Guilt twisted in her gut, but beneath it was the stark truth. This wasn't working anymore.

Adam stood in the doorway with his arms crossed. His expression was unreadable, but the tension in his shoulders and the sharp set of his jaw told her everything she needed to know. He was barely holding it together. Seeing him like that made something ache in her chest, but she pushed it down.

"I'll come back for the rest of my things another day," she said, keeping her voice even.

Adam's eyes darkened. "When, Ruby? After you've had your fix of Eddie?"

Her breath caught, her fingers tightening on the suitcase handle. "Adam, I..." She hesitated, searching for the right words. "I know I messed up. I know I hurt you. But I couldn't take it anymore. The anxiety, the paranoia, always looking over our shoulders. It was exhausting."

His voice was rough. "I tried to give you everything. I did everything I could to make you feel safe."

"You didn't keep me safe from you," Ruby shot back before she could stop herself. She swallowed hard and shook her head. "I needed more than what you could give. Eddie makes me feel safe. He sees me. That's what a real man does."

The words hit him like a blow.

Adam felt the heat of anxiety rush through him, his chest rising and falling sharply. His throat bobbed like he was trying to force something back.

For a second, Ruby wanted him to yell, to fight, to do something other than stand there with that hollow look in his eyes. But he just stared at her like he didn't know her anymore.

She turned away.

Stepping outside, the morning sun hit her face, too bright, too sharp. The warmth should have been comforting, but all she felt was cold inside. She had chosen this, hadn't she? Chosen to walk away, to start over, to be with someone who didn't come with ghosts and shadows.

But as she walked down the path, suitcase rolling behind her, she couldn't shake the weight pressing down on her chest. She had wanted more. Needed more.

And yet, as she left Adam standing in the doorway, alone in the home they had built together, she wondered if she'd ever truly find it.

CHAPTER 20

Jerry pulled into Adam's driveway, shutting off the engine before stepping out. The house looked the same as always, but something felt different. He walked up to the door and knocked.

"Adam?"

A few seconds later, the door opened. Adam stood there, his expression unreadable, his shoulders tense. Without a word, he stepped aside, letting Jerry in.

Jerry took one look at him and knew something was wrong. "What happened?"

Adam let out a slow breath, rubbing his hands together before crossing his arms. "Ruby's gone. Packed her stuff and left." His voice was steady, but there was an edge to it. "Said she couldn't deal with my anxiety anymore."

Jerry frowned. "Damn. I knew things were rough, but I didn't think she'd actually leave."

Adam's jaw tightened. "She didn't just leave." He looked Jerry in the eye, his tone sharp. "She's been seeing Eddie."

Jerry scoffed. "Eddie Calahan? That loser? The guy who sat on unemployment for two years and got fired from the gas station?"

"Yeah. That Eddie."

Jerry shook his head in disbelief. "Damn. Did you know it was him before she admitted it?"

Adam exhaled, his fingers tightening slightly around his arms. "I had a feeling. Saw them talking at the supermarket a few times. Nothing obvious, but something just felt off. The way she looked at him, how she got quiet when she saw me."

Adam took a few deep breaths to calm himself down before continuing. "Guess she wanted someone who didn't give a damn about keeping her safe. Thought I was doing everything right, but apparently, that wasn't enough."

Jerry leaned against the wall, arms crossed. "You didn't deserve that. No way in hell. And it sure as hell ain't on you."

Adam exhaled through his nose. "Doesn't feel that way."

Jerry clapped a firm hand on his shoulder. "Come on. Let's get out of here for a while. Grab some breakfast, clear your head."

Adam hesitated before nodding. "Yeah. Alright."

Before they left, Jerry glanced around and asked Adam, "Where's Fletcher?"

"I had my uncle pick him up," Adam replied. "Didn't want him around if there's a Dogman nearby."

"Makes sense," Jerry said with a nod. "The boys went to their mom's this morning. Easier to concentrate when I know they're safe."

The drive to the diner was quiet. Jerry didn't push, and Adam wasn't in the mood to talk. When they arrived, the familiar scent of coffee and bacon hit them as they walked inside. A waitress led them to a booth near the window and handed them menus.

Adam didn't bother looking at his. "Pancakes. Scrambled eggs. Thanks."

Jerry ordered a full platter. When their food arrived, Adam barely touched his, absently pushing the pancakes around with his fork.

Jerry watched him before setting his own fork down. "You need to eat, man."

Adam picked up a piece of pancake, chewing without tasting it. "I don't even know what to do next. Lost my wife and kid, thought I was finally getting my life back on track, and now this." He shook his head. "I never thought she'd cheat on me."

Jerry leaned forward, his tone firm. "I didn't either. But listen, you're not gonna let this break you. I've got your back, and we'll figure it out. One step at a time."

Adam nodded, finally taking another bite. It didn't change anything, but at least he wasn't sitting alone in that house. He had been through worse. He wasn't about to let this take him down.

CHAPTER 21

Sheriff Walters walked into the diner, his face lined with exhaustion. The usual morning hum of conversation quieted as he passed, his presence drawing attention. He spotted Adam and Jerry in their usual booth and made his way over, pulling out a chair with a sigh.

"Morning, Sheriff," Jerry greeted, eyeing him. "Rough night?"

"You could say that," the sheriff said, rubbing his temple. "One of the busiest nights I've had in a long time."

Adam set his coffee down. "We heard about the collision out on Old Mill Road. Came over the scanner last night."

Jerry nodded. "Yeah, Adam told me. Sounded bad."

Sheriff Walters let out a breath. "It was. One driver was

killed on impact, but the other…" He hesitated before continuing. "The other was dead when we got there but she was mauled. Badly."

Adam and Jerry sat up straighter, their expressions shifting from concern to shock.

"You're saying you think the Dogman attacked her *after* the accident?" Adam asked, his voice firm.

"That's what it looks like," Walters confirmed. "She was still in the driver's seat, windshield busted in, torn up in a way that sure as hell wasn't from the crash. We all know what's out there."

Jerry let out a low whistle. "Damn."

"And that wasn't even the worst of it," Sheriff Walters continued, rubbing the back of his neck. "Chris Menaro got attacked. He made it, but he's messed up. Got released from the hospital this morning, but he's going to need time to recover."

"Chris?" Jerry's eyebrows lifted. "Didn't even know he was back in town."

"He wasn't planning on making a big deal out of it, I guess," Sheriff Walters said. "But yeah, he had a run-in. He's lucky to be alive."

Adam clenched his jaw. "This is insane."

Walters shook his head. "And there is one more. Some guy trying to steal a catalytic converter off Doug Hindmarsh's truck didn't make it."

Jerry exhaled, running a hand through his hair. "Three attacks in one night?"

"Looks like it," Sheriff Walters said, his voice tight. "We're doing everything we can to track it, but you know how that goes."

Adam drummed his fingers against the table, his mind racing. "Can we see Chris? I'd like to check in on him."

Walters nodded. "Call him first. He's shaken up, and I don't know if he's up for visitors yet."

Jerry shook his head. "This is starting to feel a lot like last time."

Adam exhaled sharply. "Yeah. Except worse."

Sheriff Walters checked his watch. "I need to touch base with the FBI, see what the hell they were doing while all this was happening. But right now, I'm on my way to have a quick chat with the man who called the crash into 911 last night. I'll find out if he saw anything." He stood, adjusting his belt.

"Keep your eyes open. If you see anything, call me. And don't try to handle this yourselves."

Adam and Jerry both nodded.

The sheriff turned toward the door, but before he could take a step, his radio crackled to life.

"Sheriff, we've got a report from a woman on Maple Drive. Says she thinks there's a dead body in her rose bushes."

Sheriff Walters closed his eyes for half a second before keying the radio. "Copy that. I'm on my way."

He looked back at Adam and Jerry, his face unreadable. "Looks like my morning just got even longer." Without another word, he walked out, heading toward his cruiser.

Jerry let out a slow breath, shaking his head. "Another one? That thing went on a freakin' rampage last night!"

Adam stared at his plate, appetite long gone. "I was hoping the FBI was going to take it out before it could attack more people. Guess not."

Jerry grabbed his coffee, taking a long sip. "Yeah, so much for their freakin' help. Four attacks in one freakin' night. That's insane."

CHAPTER 22

Sheriff Walters walked briskly to his cruiser, his mind already shifting to the next crisis. The report had just come through, a woman had called in about what looked like a dead body in her rose bushes. He climbed into the driver's seat, started the engine, and pulled onto the road, the seriousness of the call pressing against his already frayed nerves.

As he drove, he grabbed his radio. "Rodriguez, you en route to Maple Drive?"

"Already ahead of you, Sheriff," came the deputy's reply. "I'll secure the scene."

"Good. I'll be there in a few minutes," Sheriff Walters said. He needed answers. He dialed a number he had come to know all too well.

After two rings, a voice answered. "Special Agent Johnson."

"Special Agent Johnson, it's Sheriff Walters," he said firmly. "Where the hell was your team last night? We had more attacks. Two people are dead, one man is injured and now I'm on my way to check out another body."

There was a pause. "Sheriff, we were called away on an urgent assignment. It couldn't be helped. We'll be back in a few days."

Sheriff Walters clenched his jaw. "You're telling me that with everything going on here, the FBI just packed up and left? We have a goddamn creature tearing through this town, and I can't exactly put out a press release saying 'don't worry, the feds will be back soon.'"

Johnson's voice remained level. "I understand your frustration, Sheriff, but we have to prioritize resources. This other case required immediate attention."

"That's not good enough," Sheriff Walters snapped. "You told me you were here to handle this. Now we've got a rising body count and a town full of scared people. How much worse does it have to get before you stick around?"

"We're coming back as soon as we can," Johnson said, his

tone firm. "Until then, I suggest you keep your deputies on high alert. Take every precaution necessary."

Sheriff Walters exhaled through his nose, barely keeping his temper in check. "Fine. But when you get back, you better come ready for war, because this thing isn't slowing down."

"We'll be in touch," Johnson said before the line went dead.

Sheriff Walters tossed the phone onto the passenger seat with a mumbled curse. He was on his own. Again.

His phone buzzed, Mary's name flashing on the screen. He took a sharp breath in before answering.

"Hey, sweetheart," Mary's familiar voice greeted him.

"Hey, Mary," he replied, working to keep his voice steady. "How are you and Maddie?"

"We're good. Just baking some cookies. How are things over there?"

He took a slow breath. "Listen, Mary, I need you to do something for me. I need you and Maddie to go stay with Selina for a few days."

A pause. "Why, Scott? What's going on?"

He hesitated before choosing his words. "It's not safe right now."

Mary's voice dropped. "Scott, what aren't you telling me?"

"I can't get into details," he admitted. "But trust me. You and Maddie need to be away from town until this settles down."

"Is it really that bad?" she asked, the worry in her voice unmistakable.

He glanced at the road ahead. "Bad enough that I'm asking you to do this."

A long silence stretched between them before Mary finally sighed. "Alright. If it'll give you peace of mind, we'll go. But promise me you'll be careful."

"I promise," he said, some of the weight easing from his chest. "Thank you, Mary. I love you."

"I love you too," she murmured. "We'll pack and leave by lunch."

The sheriff ended the call, his stomach still twisted in knots. He had to keep his family safe. He had to keep *everyone* safe.

As he pulled onto Maple Drive, he spotted Rodriguez's

cruiser parked near a modest brick home. An older woman stood on the porch, her arms folded tightly, watching them approach.

Sheriff Walters took a breath, bracing himself. The night had been hell, and from the look of things, the morning wasn't going to be any better.

CHAPTER 23

Ruby sat on the worn-out couch in Eddie's cluttered living room, her suitcase still by the door. The place smelled of stale beer and cheap cologne, with old magazines, dirty laundry, and empty takeout containers scattered around. It was nothing like the home she had shared with Adam, but right now, she needed to be away from him.

Eddie sprawled next to her, tossing an arm over the back of the couch. "So, you finally broke free," he said, grinning. "Figured you'd had enough of Captain Doom and Gloom."

Ruby exhaled, rubbing her temples. "Don't be an ass, Eddie."

He snorted. "Come on, babe. The guy was wound tighter than a damn clock. Bet he even locked the fridge at night."

A small smile tugged at Ruby's lips, but she shook her

head. "Adam's a good man. He just worries too much and is always preparing for the worst. I couldn't live like that anymore. I want to feel normal, to live without fear."

Eddie stretched, kicking an empty beer can across the floor. "Yeah, well, normal is what I do best. No paranoia, no werewolf nonsense. Just you, me, and whatever the hell we feel like doing."

Ruby leaned back, staring at the ceiling. "I loved him, you know. I really did."

Eddie scoffed. "Love's overrated. Look where it got you. Stressed out and babysitting a grown man's panic attacks."

She sighed, not wanting to argue. "He saw something, Eddie. Whatever happened that night at the cabin, he wasn't making it up."

Eddie waved a dismissive hand. "Yeah, yeah. Big, scary shadow. Maybe a bear, maybe some freak in a costume. Whatever it was, he let it ruin his life. And yours."

Ruby frowned, but part of her wanted to believe him. "I don't know. Maybe I let it ruin mine too."

Eddie nudged her with his knee. "Well, you're here now, and that means a fresh start. No more drama. Just us."

She wanted that to be true. She needed it to be true.

Eddie flashed her his signature smirk. "Besides, once I get that payout from the service station, we're golden. No more scraping by. We can do whatever we want."

Ruby raised an eyebrow. "And when is this magical payday happening?"

"Soon," he said with confidence. "Couple more weeks, tops."

She wanted to trust that, just like she wanted to trust him.

Eddie leaned in, lowering his voice. "And don't worry about Adam. He'll get over it. You made the right choice, babe."

Ruby hesitated but eventually nodded. "Yeah... I hope so."

He pulled her closer, and Ruby let herself sink into the comfort of his embrace, shoving aside the nagging doubt that whispered beneath the surface. Right now, she just needed to believe she had made the right decision.

CHAPTER 24

Adam sat on his couch, gripping his phone, his thoughts tangled in frustration and worry. He took a deep breath before dialing Chris's number, hoping his friend could give him some insight into what had happened the night before.

"Hey, Chris, it's Adam," he said when Chris picked up. "Can we come over? We need to talk to you about what happened."

Chris didn't hesitate. "Yeah, man. Come on over."

Adam called Jerry, and within minutes, they were on the road. As the truck rumbled down the quiet streets, they were both lost in their own thoughts.

When they pulled up to Chris's house, the front door opened before they even knocked. Chris stood in the doorway, looking pale and exhausted, one arm moving stiffly as he waved them inside.

Adam stepped in first. "Appreciate you seeing us. We heard about the attack. You alright?"

Chris lowered himself onto the couch with a wince. "Could've been worse. Just a slash across my back. It's deep, but I'll live."

Jerry pulled up a chair. "Damn, man. I didn't even know you were back in town."

Chris let out a tired breath. "Got back a couple weeks ago. Job didn't work out up in Junee."

Jerry nodded. "That sucks. Glad you're back though, even if it's under shitty circumstances."

Chris gave a half-hearted chuckle. "Yeah, tell me about it."

Jerry leaned forward. "Can you tell us exactly what happened?"

Chris ran a hand through his hair. "I was just walking home as normal. I looked up and saw it at the end of the street. This thing was huge, covered in dark fur, with these insane glowing amber eyes. At first, I thought it was some guy in a costume or maybe a big-ass dog standing funny, but then it moved, and I knew."

Adam and Jerry exchanged a glance, already knowing

what was coming.

Chris's voice dropped. "It looked straight at me. Like it was thinking. I panicked and ran. The thing came after me. I could hear its footsteps pounding behind me, and before I could react, it slashed my back. I stumbled but then a car came down the road and I guess spooked it cause it took off. I saw an alley and ran into it."

Chris leaned forward, rubbing his forehead. "I crawled behind a dumpster and I thought it had me cause it was sniffing the air. I guess after a few minutes it lost interest and ran off. I've never run so fast to get home before and I've definitely never felt so freakin' scared in my life."

Jerry let out a low breath. "You're so lucky, man."

"What exactly did it look like?" Adam asked.

Chris's expression darkened. "Wolf face, but bigger and longer. Wrong, somehow. Long teeth, huge claws. It stood on two legs but moved like it wasn't supposed to. And..." He hesitated before continuing. "I think it was female. You could see nipples down its chest where it was missing hair. But those eyes, man. They weren't just wild animal eyes. They knew."

Adam ran a hand down his face. "There's something you need to know, Chris. Last year, Jerry and I were at my cabin.

We killed a Dogman that had been terrorizing me. It had killed Dan Ludlow, my neighbor."

Chris's eyebrows shot up. "Dan? I thought a bear got him."

Adam shook his head. "That's what they told people. But it wasn't a bear. It was a Dogman."

Chris sat back, gripping his knees. "So now another one is out there?"

Adam nodded. "Looks that way. And anyone who gets in its path is in trouble."

Jerry crossed his arms. "You need to keep your family safe. Either get out of town for a bit or don't step outside at night. If it's got your scent, it won't forget it."

Chris let out a slow breath. "Jesus. I think we'll go to my brother's place in Fischer for a week or two. Just to be safe."

Adam gave a nod. "That's smart."

They stayed for a few more minutes, making sure Chris was holding up before heading back to the truck.

As they climbed in, Adam looked over at Jerry. "I'll drop you off, then see you at my place before sunset. We need to be prepared before nightfall."

Jerry gave a firm nod. "Good call. I'll be there."

Adam started the engine. "Gonna stop by the store, grab enough supplies to last us a few days. I don't want to have to go out again once the sun sets."

"Good idea," Jerry said, his worried gaze fixed on the road ahead.

CHAPTER 25

Sheriff Walters pulled onto a side road, his mind still reeling from what he'd just left behind. The coroner had all but confirmed it, another Dogman attack.

The blood trail painted a clear picture. The man had been knocked from his bike, dragged into the bushes, and torn apart. The Dogman had fed, just like it had with the woman in the car crash.

The body count was climbing, and so was Walters' blood pressure.

He took a slow breath, steadying himself before grabbing the radio. "Dispatch, this is Sheriff Walters. I need an emergency SMS alert sent townwide. Effective immediately."

A brief pause. Then, "Copy that, Sheriff. What's the

message?"

He kept it direct. "Large, extremely dangerous animal on the loose. Residents are advised to stay indoors after dark and ensure all doors and windows are secured. Do not attempt to approach or engage with any wildlife acting aggressively. Report any suspicious activity to law enforcement immediately."

"Understood. I'll have it sent out within the next few minutes."

"Good. Also, have the Admin team post the same notice across all department social media channels. If people won't read a text, maybe they'll read a post."

"Will do, Sheriff."

Setting the radio down, Walters watched parents stroll with their children, a sigh escaping his lips. While they laughed and smiled, a storm raged within him.

The FBI still hadn't given him any solid answers on when they would be back, and until they did, all he could do was try to keep the town from losing any more lives.

He had done the only thing he could for now—warn the townsfolk and hope to God they listened.

CHAPTER 26

Adam walked into the grocery store, his mind focused on the supplies he needed. Grabbing a cart, he moved through the aisles, methodically stocking up on frozen meals, bottled water, and other essentials to last a few days. Preparation was key since he had no idea how long this situation would drag on. Besides, keeping busy was better than dwelling on everything else.

As he turned down the canned goods aisle, he caught sight of Eddie Calahan near the end, casually browsing the shelves. Adam's heart sank. The last thing he wanted was to confront the man Ruby had cheated with, especially now, with everything else going on.

He tried to stay clear of Eddie, hoping to finish his shopping unnoticed. But luck wasn't on his side. Just as Adam was about to turn into the next aisle, Eddie looked up and saw him. A smirk spread across Eddie's face, and he walked over, his confidence apparent in every step.

"Well, well, if it isn't Captain Doom and Gloom," Eddie said, stopping a few feet away. "Fancy seeing you here."

Adam ran a head over his face, forcing himself to stay calm. "Eddie."

Eddie leaned against the shelves, his smirk widening. "How's it going? Ruby's settling in nicely, in case you were wondering."

Adam felt a surge of anger but took a deep breath to keep it in check. "I wasn't, actually."

Eddie chuckled, clearly enjoying the tension. "You know, Adam, you really should learn to let go. Holding on to grudges isn't good for you."

"I'm not interested in your advice, Eddie," Adam replied, his voice low and controlled. "I'm just here to get supplies and go home."

Eddie raised an eyebrow, looking mockingly thoughtful. "Supplies, huh? Preparing for the apocalypse or something?"

Adam met Eddie's gaze, his eyes hard. "Just being prepared."

Eddie shrugged, still smirking. "Whatever you say, man. Just remember, Ruby made her choice. You're just gonna have to live with it."

Adam's fists clenched around the cart handle, but he refused to let Eddie provoke him further. "I'm done here. Stay out of my way, Eddie."

Without waiting for a response, Adam turned and walked away, his heart pounding with a mix of anger and hurt. He finished his shopping as quickly as possible, avoiding any further encounters. As he loaded the groceries into his car, he couldn't shake the frustration that Eddie's words had stirred.

Driving home, Adam tried to refocus his thoughts on the pressing matters at hand. The Dogman was too close for comfort. But Eddie's taunts lingered in his mind, a reminder of the betrayal and the pain that was still too raw.

As he pulled into his driveway, Adam took a deep breath, forcing himself to let go of the anger. He had more important things to worry about. He needed to protect his home, his friends, and himself. Eddie Calahan was just a distraction he couldn't afford.

Adam carried the supplies inside, steeling himself for the night ahead. The real threat was out there in the darkness, and he needed to stay focused. There would be time to deal with the hurt later. For now, survival was the only thing that mattered.

CHAPTER 27

Sheriff Walters had just left Darren Holt's house, the witness to last night's car crash. Darren described how he had driven past the wreckage, planning to stop, but froze at the sight of a creature, something straight out of a nightmare, tearing into the victim. Fear took hold, and he hit the gas, speeding away.

The sheriff already suspected the Dogman had found the crash site and finished off the woman, but Darren's account only confirmed it.

Now, he was heading home, hoping to catch a few hours of sleep before the chaos started up again. Just as he turned onto his street, his phone rang.

Dr Purtell, the coroner.

Sheriff Walters sighed as he answered. "Tell me you've got

something useful, Doc."

"I do," Purtell replied, her tone serious. "My assistant just finished the full exam on the woman from the crash. I reviewed the findings and signed off on it."

Sheriff Walters kept his eyes on the road. "And?"

"There's no doubt about it," Purtell said. "She was attacked by a large predator. The bite radius is massive, bigger than anything a wolf, bear or cougar could manage. Claw wounds are deep, some straight through muscle to the bone. And Sheriff, she was alive when it happened."

The sheriff exhaled sharply. "Damn it."

"She had defensive wounds. Scratches on the interior of the car, signs she was trying to get free. But whatever did this, it was already on her before she had a chance."

Sheriff Walters let that settle for a moment before asking, "Did she die quickly?"

Purtell hesitated. "Hard to say. But her throat was crushed. That's what finished her. That said, the injuries from the crash were severe. Even if she hadn't been attacked, she wouldn't have survived long. The attack sped up what was already inevitable."

The sheriff shook his head. "So, it wasn't just an attack. It was a kill."

"Yeah," Purtell said grimly. "And it wasn't just a kill. The wounds are consistent with feeding."

Sheriff Walters rubbed a hand over his face, exhaustion creeping in. "That's interesting," he said. "It went after her while she was still alive, but it didn't touch the other body. Didn't even seem interested in the already dead person."

Purtell was quiet for a moment. "Yeah. That stood out to me too. If it was just scavenging, it would have taken what was easiest. But this thing wanted the living one. Maybe instilling fear in its victims is part of the thrill?"

The sheriff tapped his fingers against the wheel. "Like it prefers the hunt over the actual killing."

"Looks that way," Purtell admitted.

"There's more," she added after a pause. "I took a preliminary look at the body found in the bushes. Still have to do a full exam, but like I said at the scene, the injuries match. Same bite pattern, same type of claw wounds. And all of them are consistent with the attack in Carlisle the other morning."

The sheriff pulled into his driveway. "You saying we're dealing with the same creature?"

Purtell sighed. "Best guess? Yeah. The size, the damage, the way it attacks, it all matches."

Sheriff Walters stared at his front door. "Well, at least we are dealing with only one.

"I'd say so," Purtell said.

Purtell sighed. "I'll finish up here and get you a full report, but Sheriff, I am sure you know this thing won't stop on its own."

The sheriff didn't need to be told that. He glanced at the clock on his dash, the afternoon light offering a false sense of peace.

"No, it won't," he said.

CHAPTER 28

On the outskirts of town, deep within the woods, stood an old, abandoned house. The paint had long since peeled away, leaving the wooden boards to rot and decay. Windows were shattered, and the roof sagged, but the house still stood as a silent sentinel in the wilderness. Inside, darkness reigned, and it was here that the Dogman had found refuge.

Throughout the day, the Dogman had been holed up in a small, dank room at the back of the house. The smell of mold and decay filled the air, but she didn't mind. She had spent the daylight hours in a state of restless slumber, her ears twitching at every creak and groan of the old building.

As dusk approached, she stirred. Stretching her powerful limbs, claws scraping against the wooden floor, she slowly opened her eyes. The dim light of the setting sun filtered through the broken windows, painting the walls in strange patterns. Her eyes glowed faintly, reflecting the last remnants of daylight as she rose to her full height.

She moved silently through the house, padded feet gliding over creaky floorboards without a sound. Stopping at a shattered window, she peered out into the encroaching darkness. The night was hers, and she felt the familiar surge of power as the sun disappeared beyond the trees.

Turning away from the window, she moved deeper into the house, navigating its darkened corridors with ease.

In what had once been the living room, she paused. The room was empty except for broken furniture and the remnants of a fireplace. She stepped toward the hearth, sniffing at the cold ashes, memories of her sibling flashing through her mind. The anger inside her deepened.

A low growl rumbled from her throat. Tonight, she would begin her hunt in earnest.

With a final glance around the abandoned house, she was just about to leave when she heard the clumsy shuffle of footsteps and the sound of voices slurring together.

Two hairless ones stumbled through the front door, eyes darting around the darkness. Their clothes were filthy and torn, their movements jittery with withdrawal.

"Come on, let's find a spot and get this over with," the male said, voice shaking.

The female hesitated, looking around nervously. "I don't like this, Tim. It feels… wrong."

"Just shut up and keep moving," Tim snapped, pulling her further inside.

The Dogman watched from the shadows, her glowing eyes narrowing. Their scent—fear, sweat, desperation—only fueled her anger. She had no interest in them at first, but they had wandered too close. They had entered her den.

The female slowed near the doorway of the room where she had been sleeping, her instincts screaming at her. "Tim, we shouldn't be here."

Tim turned to snap at her again, but his words died in his throat as the Dogman emerged from the darkness.

The female screamed, the sound sharp and shrill in the empty house. Tim stumbled back, gasping. "What the fuck is that?!"

The Dogman didn't hesitate.

Her claws shot out, raking across his chest before he could

react. Blood sprayed onto the broken floorboards. As he clutched the wound, she grabbed his leg and yanked hard. His hip joint popped with a sickening crack, his body twisting unnaturally.

He barely had time to choke out a gurgled sound before her jaws clamped over his face. The scream he might have let out was swallowed by the wet crunch of bone.

The female turned to run, but she was too slow. The Dogman caught her easily, jerking her backward with brutal force. She shrieked, twisting in her grasp, nails scraping uselessly against thick fur.

"Please! No!" Her voice broke as she sobbed. "Someone help me!"

There was no one to help.

She struggled, but the Dogman didn't let go. Her claws dug in deep, anchoring her prey. Then, with the ease of a predator, she bit down hard on the back of her neck. Teeth sank into soft flesh and bone, hot blood spilling onto her tongue.

The woman went limp, her final breath rattling from her throat.

The Dogman didn't stop. She tore into the body, ripping flesh from bone with savage efficiency. The wet sounds of tearing meat filled the room as she fed, warm blood pooling beneath her. Her powerful jaws crushed through muscle and sinew, each bite fueling the fire of her rage.

When she finally lifted her head, her muzzle was slick with blood. She had fed, but the hunger remained, simmering just beneath the surface. This was only the beginning.

The real hunt was still ahead.

Slipping out through a broken door, she melted into the woods, the cool night air brushing against her fur. She moved with purpose, her body blending into the darkness.

The men responsible for her brother's death were still out there.

And before the sun rose, they would know what it meant to be hunted.

CHAPTER 29

The last traces of sunlight faded as townsfolk drove home from another long day. Adam stood on the porch, arms crossed, scanning the street for Jerry and Rick. The approaching night carried an uneasy stillness, as if something unseen lurked just beyond the glow of the streetlights.

He had been preparing for this moment for nearly a year. Every door reinforced, every window secured. There was no room for doubt. Call it instinct or just a feeling. He knew it was coming.

The low rumble of an engine broke the quiet. Jerry's truck turned into the driveway, followed closely by Rick's SUV. Adam stepped down from the porch as they parked and climbed out.

Jerry stretched his arms. "Damn, just made it."

Rick smirked. "Yeah, thanks to your slow ass."

Adam opened the door. "Let's get inside."

They moved quickly, unloading supplies, bags of food, spare clothes, extra ammunition. Jerry set a few cases of bottled water on the counter while Rick double-checked the firearms he had brought. Adam made sure the door was locked before turning to face them.

"There's something I want to show you before we settle in," Adam said, leading them into the hallway.

He gestured toward the steel-reinforced doors, running a hand over the heavy lock. "Every door in this house is reinforced. Steel core, commercial-grade deadbolts. Nothing's getting through."

Jerry ran a hand along the surface, nodding in approval. "Damn, Adam. This is solid. You weren't messing around."

Rick knocked on the frame, impressed. "Better than anything I've seen."

Adam moved to the windows. "Every window has steel bars on the inside. Custom-made. You can't see them from the street, but they're there. Shatterproof glass, too."

Jerry let out a low whistle. "This place is a fortress."

Rick grinned. "No wonder you wanted us here. If anywhere's safe, it's this house."

Adam led them toward a section of the wall in the hallway. A bookcase stood against it, looking like any ordinary shelf. He reached behind it, pressing a small panel. With a soft click, a hidden compartment slid open.

Inside was an armory—rifles, shotguns, handguns—all neatly arranged, each loaded and ready for use.

Jerry let out a slow whistle. "Now that's what I'm talking about."

Rick nodded approvingly. "Damn, man!"

Adam locked the panel back into place. "I spent months getting this right. We're not just sitting ducks here—we're prepared this time."

They returned to the living room, where they laid out their gear and checked their weapons.

Jerry leaned back in his chair, shaking his head in admiration. "Man, I wish I had half this setup at my place."

Rick smirked. "I'd say we're staying in the safest spot in the county."

Adam didn't respond right away. He grabbed his rifle,

checking the sights before setting it beside him. "We stay inside. We don't go out unless absolutely necessary."

Jerry's expression darkened. "And just wait for it?"

Adam nodded. "That's the plan."

Jerry exhaled sharply, rubbing his jaw. "I don't like sitting around while that thing's out there. We should be hunting it."

Rick shook his head. "We're better off here. If we go out looking for it, we're the ones getting hunted."

Jerry leaned forward, his voice tight. "And if it attacks someone else while we're in here waiting?"

Adam met his gaze. "You think we'd find it first? That thing has been picking people off in the dark for days. It's smart, Jerry. It knows how to avoid us."

Jerry crossed his arms, his jaw clenched. "Still doesn't sit right with me."

Rick shrugged. "I'd rather be bored sitting here waiting for it, then dead."

Adam tapped the table. "We're not just waiting. We've got eyes on everything. We stay inside, we stay alert, and if it comes for us, we take it down."

Jerry sighed, shaking his head. "Fine. I'd like to argue, but you both make too much sense."

The room settled into silence as they each mentally prepared for the night ahead. They weren't just holding out. They were standing their ground.

CHAPTER 30

The living room was dimly lit, the single lamp casting flickering light over the table where their supplies were spread out. The three men sat around it, a beer each in hand.

Rick shifted in his chair. "Why is it here? Nobody's ever reported anything like this in Hickory before. We kill one last year, and now another shows up? That doesn't feel like a coincidence."

Jerry exhaled. "Yeah. If these things were always around, surely we would have at least heard rumors about it."

Adam let that sink in before speaking. "I've got a bad feeling about this."

Rick's gaze sharpened. "Go on."

Adam's voice was steady. "I honestly think it's here

because of us."

Jerry frowned. "Why?"

Adam leaned forward. "It's like Rick said. We killed the only Dogman we'd ever heard of. Now, suddenly, there's another one? In a small town in Missouri? What are the odds?"

Rick's expression darkened. "You think this one's connected?"

Adam nodded. "Feels that way."

Jerry rubbed a hand down his face. "Hell."

Adam continued. "I have no way to prove it, of course. Just my gut telling me."

Rick crossed his arms. "If that's true, it's not just passing through. It's after *us*."

A heavy silence filled the room.

Jerry broke it first. "Then we make sure it doesn't get what it wants."

Adam met his gaze. "Damn right."

CHAPTER 31

Jason Kunze strummed his guitar, letting the melody flow through his fingers as he sat in his garage-turned-studio. The walls were lined with old concert posters and soundproofing foam, creating the perfect space to get lost in his music. He hummed softly, scribbling down lyrics in a worn notebook. This was his sanctuary, a place where nothing else mattered.

Inside the house, Helen was probably curled up with a book or watching TV, letting his music drift through the walls like she always did. She had told him more than once that it made the house feel alive. That thought brought a small smile to his lips. They had built a good life together, comfortable and steady, filled with small joys.

The garage door was open, letting in the cool night air. He

liked playing with the night around him, the quiet of the world beyond his music. His focus was so deep that he didn't notice how still the night had become. The crickets had gone silent, the breeze had died, and the usual background noise of the town had faded into nothing.

Until a low growl broke the silence.

Jason froze, his fingers stilling on the strings. His eyes flicked up, searching the darkness beyond the open garage.

Another growl, closer this time.

He set his guitar down and stood, peering past the dim glow of the garage light. His yard, usually familiar and safe, suddenly felt different.

Great. The neighbor's Rottweiler is out again, he thought.

Then, footsteps.

Heavy. Slow. Getting closer.

Jason's pulse picked up.

Too heavy for a dog.

It could be a bear, though they weren't common in town.

He reached for the garage door button, ready to close it

just in case.

Something stepped into view.

Towering on all fours, its thick, dark coat seemed to absorb the light, swallowing every trace of illumination. In the moonlight, the creature's eyes flickered, intelligent, calculating, and hinting at something far more sinister. Hunger.

Jason forgot to breathe.

Is that a freakin' werewolf?

She bared her fangs, saliva dripping from sharp teeth.

Holy shit.

For a moment, Jason's body refused to move, his mind scrambling to make sense of what he was seeing. He had heard the rumors, the whispered stories around town. But this? This was real.

And it was looking right at him.

Panic shot through his system. He lunged for the door button.

Too late.

The Dogman rushed forward, claws scraping against the concrete. Jason snatched his guitar and swung it with everything he had. The wood cracked against thick muscle, but the creature barely reacted.

Jason staggered back, tripping over an amplifier. Pain flared in his ankle, but adrenaline pushed him forward.

"Get out of here!" he shouted, voice breaking.

The Dogman snarled, a deep, rolling sound that sent a shudder through him. Fear clenched in his gut, and his body betrayed him as warmth spread down his leg.

She came for. Sudden and incredibly fast.

Jason swung again, but this time she caught his arm, claws slicing through his shirt and skin. He gasped in pain as blood immediately soaked into the fabric.

Desperate, he reached for a wrench from his toolbox and swung wildly. The metal connected with her cheek, drawing a thin trickle of dark blood.

It only made her angrier.

She swiped again, knocking the wrench from his grip. Jason crashed against a stack of amplifiers, his ribs aching from the impact.

"Help!" he choked out. "Somebody!"

Helen was inside, unaware of the nightmare unfolding just beyond the walls.

The Dogman crouched, watching him struggle. She was enjoying this.

Jason kicked out, his boot striking her knee. It was like striking a bear with a paper straw.

She grabbed him, claws digging deep, and dragged him forward. The last thing Jason saw was those glowing eyes before her jaws closed around his throat.

Blood gushed, hot and fast. The world tilted.

Everything went dark.

****

Helen sat curled up on the couch, flipping through a cozy romance novel, a guilty pleasure she rarely admitted to. The sound of Jason's guitar had stopped a while ago, but she hadn't thought much of it. He often paused to jot down lyrics, lost in thought.

Then, she heard his voice, muffled, distant.

At first, she thought he was singing, maybe working

through a melody. But when she heard it again, something in his tone made her stomach flip. He sounded panicked.

Frowning, she set her book aside and stood. She stretched before making her way toward the back door. As she stepped onto the porch, the cool air brushed against her skin.

Her eyes drifted toward the garage. The side door was open, and the light on in the garage. But something was very wrong.

A wave of panic took over her.

Jason lay sprawled on the floor, his body partially obscured by the angle of the doorway. Blood pooled around him, dark and glistening. He was facing away from her, his limbs twitching in short, jerky spasms.

Helen's mind struggled to process what she was seeing.

Then, movement.

From beyond Jason's body, something shifted in the shadows. A hulking shape rose, its head lifting into view.

A wolf's head.

But it was too large. Too unnatural. Too unreal.

The Dogman stepped forward, her dark coat swallowing

the light, her powerful jaws slick with blood. Her ears twitched, registering the hairless one's presence before its glowing amber eyes locked onto hers.

Helen couldn't move.

The world around her vanished, reduced to the space between her and the beast in the garage.

The Dogman stared at her for a long, terrifying moment before it took a slow, deliberate step toward the door.

Helen turned and bolted for the house.

She barely made it inside before slamming the door shut and locking it. Her hands fumbled with the deadbolt, tears running down her cheeks.

A low growl rumbled from outside.

Helen stumbled backward, heart hammering. She grabbed the biggest knife she could find from the kitchen drawer, her fingers trembling so badly she almost dropped it.

Glass shattered.

She turned toward the hallway in time to see claws rake through the window frame. The Dogman was inside.

Helen backed away, knife held tight, but she knew it

wouldn't matter.

The Dogman moved with slow, calculated steps. She was toying with her.

Helen tried to speak, but her throat was too tight.

She lunged with the knife, aiming for the beast's chest.

The Dogman knocked it aside effortlessly.

Helen spun, trying to flee, but claws wrapped around her arm, yanking her back. A scream died in her throat as monstrous fangs sank in, spraying blood across the kitchen floor.

By the time the Dogman slipped back into the night, Jason and Helen's bodies lay lifeless, the house silent except for a ticking clock on the wall.

It would be two days before Jason's daughter asked for a wellness check, leading police to the grisly scene.

CHAPTER 32

Chief Deputy Mark Turner was not a man easily rattled. At forty-five, with twenty years on the force, he prided himself on his skepticism and practicality. To him, talk of a Dogman was nothing more than local legend, another misidentification under duress. He was a man of facts and evidence, and until he saw it with his own eyes, he remained resolute in his disbelief.

Mark had come on shift at 6 PM, his demeanor as arrogant as ever. He considered himself the most capable officer in the department, often looking down on his colleagues and neighbors who entertained the idea of a mythical beast terrorizing Butler County. Even with the recent attacks, he was still skeptical.

As he drove through the quiet streets, his patrol car's engine humming steadily, he couldn't help but shake his head at the thought of the fear gripping the town.

"Dogman," he said to himself, smirking. "People will believe anything these days."

Mark's patrol car moved slowly, the spotlight on the side of the vehicle sweeping across yards and driveways. He was thorough in his rounds, but his motivation was more about proving a point than protecting the town from an imaginary threat.

Mark's eyes scanned the darkened houses, looking for any sign of trouble. He took pride in his work, but his arrogance often blinded him to the concerns of those he served. Tonight was no different. He was on a mission to debunk the hysteria, to show that Hickory's fears were unfounded.

He turned down Maple Street, his spotlight illuminating the neat, quiet yards. Everything seemed in order, just as he expected. Mark's mind wandered to the stories he'd heard, the frantic calls about a creature chasing them. He chuckled softly, shaking his head again.

"Must be the younger generations," he said, tapping his fingers on the steering wheel.

As he continued his patrol, Mark's radio crackled to life. "Unit Seven, this is dispatch. Any activity to report?"

"Negative, dispatch," Mark replied, his tone confident. "Just another quiet night in Hickory. No sign of our so-called Dogman."

"Copy that, Unit Seven. Stay safe out there."

"Always do," Mark said, switching off the radio.

CHAPTER 33

Leroy Chapel and Chad Burnett had been friends since high school, bonded by a shared love of shitty fast cars and the thrill of breaking the rules. On this particular night, they had planned to unwind after a long week by hitting their favorite local bar.

Chad, always the instigator, had suggested they start the evening with a few drinks. "Come on, man," he had said with a grin. "We deserve a night out. Let's blow off some steam."

Leroy had hesitated at first, knowing they both had a habit of pushing things too far. But the promise of a good time was too tempting to resist. "Alright," he had agreed, "but we keep it chill tonight, okay?"

They had arrived at the bar around nine, the place already buzzing with the weekend crowd. They found a table near the back, away from the prying eyes of the bartender who knew them too well. Chad ordered the first round, and soon the beers were flowing, their laughter filling the air.

As the night wore on, Chad pulled a small baggie from his jacket pocket and waved it in front of Leroy. "I got something to make this night even better," he said, his eyes gleaming with mischief.

Leroy's eyes widened, recognizing the telltale signs of trouble. "Man, you brought that stuff with you? Are you crazy?"

"Relax," Chad said, grinning. "Nobody's gonna know. It's just a little something to take the edge off."

Against his better judgment, Leroy gave in. The thrill of the night, combined with the alcohol, made it easy to forget the potential consequences. They slipped out to the back alley and shared the drugs, their senses heightening as the chemicals took effect.

Back inside the bar, everything seemed to glow with a new intensity. The music was louder, the women better looking and their inhibitions gone. They danced, drank, flirted and laughed, their worries forgotten.

By the time they stumbled out of the bar, the streets were quiet, the town asleep. Chad suggested they take a drive to keep the buzz going. "Let's hit the back roads," he said. "I know a place we can go to keep this party going."

Leroy, feeling invincible, agreed. They climbed into his car, Chad riding shotgun, and sped off into the night. The thrill of the drive, combined with the effects of the drugs and alcohol, made everything seem surreal.

They talked about old times, about the trouble they had gotten into as kids and the dreams they still had. As Leroy rambled his driving became more erratic. He swerved slightly, struggling to keep the car in its lane.

Chad, noticing the change, laughed. "You okay there, buddy? Maybe we should slow down a bit."

Leroy shook his head, his vision blurring. "I'm fine. Just a little tired. Let's keep going."

The night's fun was cut short when they saw the flashing lights of a patrol car in the rearview mirror. "Shit," Leroy said, his heart pounding. "Cops."

Chad's bravado faltered for a moment. "Just stay cool, man. We'll talk our way out of it."

Leroy pulled over, the car coming to a stop at the side of the road. They exchanged a nervous glance as the deputy approached, knowing that their night was about to take a very different turn.

CHAPTER 34

Chief Deputy Turner turned down Whittaker Street, his spotlight sweeping across more yards. Just as he was about to make a turn, he noticed a car swerving into the opposite lane, its headlights flashing erratically. Mark's eyes narrowed as he watched the vehicle struggle to stay in its lane.

His instincts kicked in, and he decided to investigate.

Mark activated his lights and pulled in behind the swerving car. The vehicle slowed down, then came to a stop at the side of the road. Mark parked his patrol car and stepped out, approaching the driver's side window cautiously.

The driver, a young man with disheveled hair, rolled down his window. Mark immediately noticed the smell of alcohol wafting out.

"Good evening, sir," Mark said, his tone firm. "License and registration, please."

"Uh, yeah, I don't know where they are right now," the driver mumbled, fumbling around.

Mark sighed. "I need you to step out of the vehicle." The driver mumbled something incoherent, but complied, fumbling with the door handle before finally stepping out. He swayed slightly, his eyes unfocused. Mark glanced at the passenger, a man around the same age who looked both annoyed and angry.

"Have you been drinking tonight?" Mark asked the driver.

"A little," the man slurred, attempting to steady himself.

"What is your name?" Mark asked the man. "It's Leroy, deputy. Leroy Chapel."

Mark sighed, guiding the man to the side of the road. "I thought I recognized you, Leroy. Alright, I'm going to need you to perform a few exercises for me. We need to see if you're capable of driving safely."

He proceeded to take Leroy through a series of DUI exercises. Leroy stumbled through the steps, failing to follow instructions properly. Mark's frustration grew as it became clear the driver was in no condition to be behind the wheel.

"Leroy, I'm going to have to place you under arrest for driving under the influence," Mark said, pulling out his handcuffs.

Leroy groaned, his shoulders sagging. "I'm sorry, deputy. I didn't mean to…"

"Save it. No-one drinks and drives in my town and gets away with it." Mark interrupted, cuffing Leroy and leading him to the patrol car.

As he secured Leroy in the back of his patrol car, he noticed the passenger getting out of the vehicle, slamming the door shut. The young man stomped over, his face twisted with anger.

"Hey! What the hell are you doing with my buddy?" the passenger demanded.

"Get back in the car," Mark ordered, his patience wearing thin.

"No way! This is bullshit!" the passenger shouted, stepping closer to Mark. "You can't just arrest him like that!"

Mark squared his shoulders, his hand resting on his belt. "I said, get back in the car. Now."

The passenger sneered, taking another step forward. "I know my rights deputy douchebag!"

Before Mark could react, the young man shoved him, hard. Mark stumbled back, his hand going to his taser gun instinctively. He drew it, aiming straight at the man's chest.

"Back off now or you're gonna get tased!" Mark barked, his voice echoing in the still night air.

The passenger hesitated, his eyes flashing with defiance. "You're not gonna tase me. I've done nuffin' wrong."

Mark took a deep breath, trying to keep his temper in check. "This isn't a game. Get back in the car and sit tight, or I'll add resisting arrest to your charges."

The young man laughed, a harsh, mocking sound. "Charges? For what? Standing up for my buddy?"

Mark stepped forward, closing the distance between them. "For assaulting a deputy. Last warning. Get in the car."

The passenger's face twisted with rage. "Screw you!" He lunged at Mark, swinging wildly. Mark side stepped, grabbing the young man's arm and twisting it behind his back. The passenger struggled, cursing and yelling, but Mark's grip was ironclad.

"I told you to back off," Mark growled, wrestling the young man to the ground. "Now you're under arrest."

He cuffed the passenger, hauling him to his feet. The young man glared at him, breathing heavily. "You're gonna regret this. Wait till my lawyer hears about this!"

Mark rolled his eyes, leading him to the patrol car. "Yeah, I've heard that before. What is your name?"

"It's Chad," said the passenger. "Chad what?" asked Mark.

"Chad. That is all you need to know."

"Alright," Mark said, "you'll cop a charge for failing to identify as well then."

He opened the door and shoved the young man inside, slamming it shut. Mark took a moment to catch his breath, his pulse racing. He glanced around, making sure there were no other surprises waiting in the shadows.

The night was far from over, and Mark's irritation was growing. He'd dealt with drunks and punks before, but something about this night felt different.

As he turned to head to the other car, he heard a rustling sound from the nearby bushes, but he dismissed it as a small critter, focusing on the task at hand.

He had no idea that the real danger was still lurking in the shadows, watching and waiting.

CHAPTER 35

Jerry stood up from his chair and started pacing the room. "This is crap. I just wish there was more we could do. Sitting here, feeling helpless, it's... it's torture."

"I get it, man," Adam said, his voice softening. "But right now, this is the best strategy. We need to keep our minds occupied. Let's put on a movie or play some cards."

Jerry looked at him, surprised. "A movie? Now?"

Adam shrugged. "Why not? It's better than just sitting here, waiting for something to happen."

Rick, now fully awake, sat up and stretched. "I'm in. Anything to keep the nerves at bay."

Adam picked up the remote and turned on the TV, scrolling through Netflix. "How about something light?" he suggested. "We could use a good laugh."

Jerry chuckled, albeit nervously. "Got any comedies in there?"

Adam scrolled through the options. "What about *'Superbad,' 'Anchorman,'* or *'Step Brothers.'* Any of those sound good?"

Rick nodded. "Let's go with *'Anchorman.'* We could use some ridiculous humor right now."

Jerry agreed. "Yeah, Ron Burgundy's antics might be just what we need."

They settled on 'Anchorman,' hoping to lose themselves in the absurdity of the movie. As the opening credits rolled, the three friends tried to relax, though their eyes still darted to the windows and doors every now and then.

The radio in the study crackled to life, startling them. Adam quickly muted the tv and walked into the room, turning up the volume as his anxiety grew.

"This is Unit Seven, we've got an 11-95. Suspected DUI, 10-72. Repeat, 11-95, 10-72."

Adam exchanged worried glances with Rick and Jerry. "What's an 11-95?" Jerry asked, his voice tense, now fully awake.

"Traffic stop," Adam replied. "And 10-72 means a possible DUI."

Rick nodded, understanding the unspoken implication. "Doesn't sound Dogman-related."

Adam took a deep breath, trying to steady his nerves. "No. Just a routine stop."

CHAPTER 36

Chief Deputy Turner had pulled over the swerving car on Whittaker Street. He had already arrested the driver for DUI and subdued the unruly passenger after a brief struggle. Both men now sat handcuffed in the back of his patrol car, their faces reflecting a mix of anger, fear, and frustration.

The driver's behavior suggested more than just alcohol. Drugs could be involved, and it was his duty to find out as he opened the car door.

Mark started his search methodically, shining his flashlight into every nook and cranny. He began with the glove compartment, finding nothing but a few crumpled receipts and an old map. He moved to the center console, his fingers brushing past empty soda cans and fast-food wrappers.

In the back of the cruiser, Leroy and Chad exchanged worried glances. Chad leaned closer to Leroy and whispered,

"He better not find the drugs. I can't afford to lose my job."

Leroy nodded, his eyes wide with fear. "I told you not to bring that shit, man."

Mark continued his search, oblivious to their conversation. He checked the back seat of the car, feeling around for any hidden compartments. His flashlight beam flickered as he moved it under the seats, scanning for anything suspicious.

Just as he was about to reach deeper, a rustling sound came from the nearby bushes. Mark paused, his hand gripping the flashlight tighter. He had dismissed the noise earlier, thinking it was just a raccoon, but now it seemed closer, more deliberate.

He stood up, turning his attention to the bushes. The hair on the back of his neck stood up as he strained to see through the darkness. The night was still, the only sound his own breathing and the faint hum of the patrol car's engine.

"What the hell is that?" Mark said to himself, stepping away from the car. He moved cautiously, as his flashlight darted from one shadow to another.

In the back of the cruiser, Leroy and Chad watched with growing unease. Chad, his bravado fading, whispered, "What's he doing?"

Leroy shook his head. "How the hell would I know?"

Mark approached the bushes, his eyes scanning the dense foliage. He could feel his pulse quickening, a sense of foreboding settling over him. He was just a few feet away when the rustling grew louder, more aggressive.

Before he could react, a giant shape burst from the bushes. The Dogman, her eyes glowing with menace, attacked Mark with terrifying speed. Mark barely had time to raise his flashlight before the creature was upon him.

The impact knocked him to the ground, his flashlight flying from his hand and rolling into the darkness. The Dogman's claws raked across his chest, tearing through his uniform and flesh. Mark screamed, the pain searing through his body.

In the back of the cruiser, Leroy and Chad watched in horror, their eyes wide. "Oh my god!" Chad yelled. "Is that a freakin' Werewolf?"

Leroy pressed himself against the back of the seat as he was starting to hyperventilate. "We're screwed, man. We're so screwed."

Mark struggled to fend off the Dogman, his mind unable

to process the fear he felt. He managed to draw his gun, firing a shot that grazed the creature's ear. The Dogman snarled, her eyes burning with fury, and swiped at Mark again, knocking the gun from his hand, breaking his trigger finger.

The Dogman's claws tore through Mark's side, as he screamed again, his vision blurring from the intense pain. The creature loomed over him, her breath hot and foul against his face. Mark knew he was outmatched, but his survival instincts kicked in. He tried to push the Dogman away, using every ounce of strength he had left.

In the cruiser, Chad was panicking, his voice frantic. "Do something! We have to help him!"

Leroy shook his head, his face drenched in sweat. "What the hell are we supposed to do? We're handcuffed, you idiot! We can't do shit!"

Mark fumbled for his radio, his fingers slick with blood. He managed to press the button, his voice a desperate whisper. "Dispatch... 11-99... officer needs help..."

The Dogman let out a roar, her fangs inches from Mark's throat. It seemed to savor the moment, the fear and helplessness in his eyes. Then, with a final, brutal swipe, she ended his struggle by slicing off most of his face. Mark's body went limp, the life draining from him as the Dogman's teeth tore through his face.

The Dogman stood over Mark's lifeless body, her breath coming in deep, satisfied huffs. It had proven her dominance, her existence, and now she sniffed the air and turned her attention to the patrol car. The two men inside watched with absolute fear in their eyes as the creature approached, her eyes locked onto them with a voracious intensity.

"Oh hell no," Leroy whispered, his voice trembling. "It's coming for us."

Chad kicked at the door, panic overwhelming him. "We have to get out of here!"

The Dogman reached the patrol car, her claws scraping against the metal. She peered through the window at them, one by one. The men inside could see every detail of her monstrous face, every sharp fang and the blood dripping from her chops.

She bared her teeth, her growl low and incredibly deep. She raised an oversized paw and slammed it against the window, the glass shuddering under the force. The men inside screamed, their fear in overdrive as the Dogman continued her assault.

"Help! Somebody fucking help us!" Chad yelled, his voice

cracking with terror.

The Dogman snarled, determined to reach the men inside. Leroy pressed himself as far away from the door as possible, his heart beating so fast he thought it would give out any second. He knew they were trapped, that there was no escape from the nightmare unfolding before them.

With a final, devastating blow, the Dogman shattered the window. Glass rained down on the men inside, cutting into their skin. The Dogman reached through the broken window, its claws closing around Chad's arm. He screamed, the pain excruciating as the creature yanked him towards the opening. Leroy watched in fear, unable to reach out and try to pull him back.

"Help me! Help me!" Chad cried, his voice raw with terror he never knew existed.

The Dogman pulled Chad through the broken window, her jaws closing around his neck. Leroy could do nothing but watch as the creature tore into his friend, the sound of ripping flesh and bone filling the air. Blood sprayed across the exterior of the cruiser, the metallic scent mingling with the stench of fear and death.

Leroy pressed himself against the far door, straining desperately against the handcuffs. Pain seared through his wrists as the metal bit into his skin, tearing it open and drawing blood. He knew he was next, that there was no escape from the creature's wrath. He closed his eyes, praying for a miracle, but none came.

The Dogman finished with Chad, her eyes gleaming with evil mischief as she turned slowly to face Leroy.

The creature reached into the cruiser again, her claws closing around Leroy's arm. He screamed, the pain blinding as the Dogman yanked him towards the opening. The last thing Leroy saw was the creature's yellowed teeth, before everything went black.

The Dogman stood over the ruined patrol car, feeling a mixture of satisfaction and faint sorrow now the fear had dissipated from her victims.

She licked her blood-soaked paw before retreating into the night, searching for more prey.

CHAPTER 37

After the movie ended, Adam was sitting in his study, his eyes heavy from the lack of sleep. The radio on his desk crackled to life, jolting him in his chair.

"Dispatch... 11-99... officer needs help..."

Adam's heart skipped a beat. That was Mark's voice. Urgent, desperate. He could tell by the sound of his voice alone that Mark was in trouble. He thought of many possibilities, none of them good.

He quickly stood up and made his way to the living room where Jerry and Rick were resting on the couch and armchair. Adam shook Jerry's shoulder gently. "Jerry, wake up. We've got a problem."

Jerry groaned and opened his eyes, blinking against the dim light. "What is it?"

"Chief Deputy Turner just called in for help. He needs urgent assistance."

Jerry sat up, instantly alert. "Where?"

"Whittaker Street. He's in trouble. I could hear it in his voice."

Rick, who had been dozing off in the armchair, sat up as well, rubbing his eyes. "What's going on?"

"Chief Deputy Turner's in trouble," Adam explained. "He called for help."

Rick looked concerned. "Should we go help him?"

Adam hesitated. Every instinct told him to go, but another part of him, the part that had survived the first Dogman attack, was screaming to stay put.

"Shit. I don't know," Adam admitted. "If it's the Dogman… it could be trying to lure us out."

Jerry's eyes widened with realization. "You think it's a trap?"

"It's possible," Adam said, running a hand through his hair. "As much as I want to run out of here guns blazing, we can't afford to take chances. We need to stay put and make sure the house is secure. If we leave, we could be walking right into an ambush."

Rick nodded, understanding the logic but hating it. "But Mark…"

Adam placed a hand on Rick's shoulder. "I know. But if we go out there, we might end up like him. Or worse. We have to think about our safety first. I am sure half the Sheriff's department is responding right now."

Jerry nodded slowly, understanding the logic but hating it. "Alright. We stay put."

Adam headed to the kitchen. "I'll make us some coffee. We need to stay awake and alert."

As Adam brewed the coffee, the aroma filled the house, offering a small comfort amidst the turmoil. He poured three cups and brought them back to the living room, handing them to Jerry and Rick.

"Thanks," Jerry said, taking a sip. "We're going to need this."

Rick nodded, cradling the cup in his hands. "Yeah, this is going to be a long night."

As the minutes ticked by, Adam couldn't shake the feeling of dread that had settled in his chest. He hoped that Mark would be alright, that backup would arrive in time to help him.

CHAPTER 38

Sheriff Walters had been out patrolling, his thoughts drifting to his wife and kids. His children were grown now, living their own lives, but he still worried about them. Nights like this made him wish he were home, sitting at the kitchen table with Mary instead of out here, chasing monsters. Then, the radio crackled to life, snapping him out of his thoughts and pulling him back into the reality of his job.

"Dispatch to all units, possible 10-71 on Whittaker Street. Chief Deputy Turner requesting immediate backup."

A bad feeling settled deep in his gut. Turner wouldn't call for backup unless it was serious.

He grabbed the radio. "Sheriff en route."

His cruiser roared as he pushed the accelerator, the quiet town blurring past.

"Davis and Cantrell, what's your ETA?" the dispatcher asked.

"Three minutes," Davis responded. "Just dropped off a transport at the jail. Heading out now."

Sheriff Walters took the last turn onto Whittaker Street, headlights cutting through the dimming light. As the scene came into view, his stomach clenched.

Turner's patrol car was parked on the side of the road, lights flashing. At first glance, everything appeared normal, except for the complete absence of life.

He killed the engine and grabbed his rifle from the cruiser.

Stepping out, he scanned the area, his eyes focussing.

"Turner?" His voice was low but firm.

Silence.

He moved closer. The metallic scent of blood thickened in the air.

Then, his flashlight beam landed on the body.

Turner lay sprawled beside a car, uniform torn, his face missing. Blood pooled beneath him, sinking into the cracks of the pavement.

Sheriff Walters forced down the rising nausea as his gaze lingered on the mangled remains of his deputy, the place where his face should have been now a raw, gaping void.

This wasn't a struggle. This was a slaughter.

He swept the beam farther.

Two more bodies lay near the cruiser.

The sheriff barely noticed the sirens approaching. A moment later, red and blue lights bathed the street as Deputies Davis and Cantrell pulled up, their patrol car screeching to a halt.

They stepped out, weapons drawn, faces dropping as they took in the scene.

"Oh, hell," Davis said.

Cantrell exhaled sharply. "Oh shit. It got Turner?"

Sheriff Walters didn't look away from the carnage. "Yes."

Davis shook his head. "This is un-fucking-believable."

Walters gave a sharp nod. "Cantrell, secure the area. Davis, check for any more victims. And watch your backs."

As they moved through the area, the radio buzzed with

updates from ambulances converging on Whittaker Street. The sense of urgency and danger was clear, and everyone knew they were up against something far more dangerous than a typical suspect.

"Sheriff, over here!" Cantrell called out, her voice tense.

Sheriff Walters and Davis hurried over to where Cantrell was pointing. In the beam of her flashlight, they saw deep gouges in the ground and blood splatters leading into a yard.

Sheriff Walters' heart pounded. "Make sure you note it."

Davis looked around nervously. "This is outta control sheriff. We really need the FBI here already. We can't handle this alone."

The sheriff nodded. "Agreed. I'll call them again. You two keep searching for any more evidence."

He grabbed his radio, his voice steady but urgent. "Dispatch, this is Sheriff Walters. We have confirmed signs of a large, hostile creature. Notify the Coroner and advise all units to proceed with extreme caution."

The dispatcher's voice crackled back. "Copy that, Sheriff. I will call the Coroner and inform all EMT's to proceed with caution. Stay safe out there."

Sheriff Walters clipped the radio back to his belt, his mind spinning. They were up against a monster, and they had to find it before it could strike again. As he looked down the dark, foreboding street, he knew this was just the beginning of a long and dangerous night.

"Stay sharp, everyone," Sheriff Walters said, his voice firm. "We're not just hunting a killer. We're hunting a monster. And we need to be ready for anything."

CHAPTER 39

The scanner crackled in the dimly lit room, each burst of static holding their attention. Adam, Jerry, and Rick sat in tense silence, listening intently to the sheriff's voice.

"That doesn't sound good," Rick said, rubbing his jaw.

Adam nodded, his thoughts racing. "If Walters is calling for the coroner and warning EMTs to be on alert, it means the Dogman attacked again."

Jerry exhaled, shifting in his seat. "Should we go help?"

Before Adam could answer, his phone rang, cutting through the heightened atmosphere. Seeing *Sheriff Walters* on the screen, he answered immediately.

"Sheriff, what's going on?"

"Adam, it struck again," Walters said, his voice rough with

exhaustion. "Mark's down. Two others are dead too."

Adam clenched his jaw.. "Jesus. Anything we can do?"

"Yeah. Stay put," Walters said firmly. "I don't know if it's here for you or not, but it's in town again tonight. You and your friends need be ready in case it shows up. Keep the house locked down and don't take any chances."

"We're ready," Adam assured him. "The house is locked down, we're armed, and we won't be caught off guard."

"Good," Walters said. "I'll keep you updated. Just stay sharp."

As the call ended, Adam turned to the others, his expression grim. "It was the Dogman. Mark's dead, two others too."

Jerry swore under his breath. "Damn it."

Rick rubbed the back of his neck. "So what now?"

Adam tightened his grip on his rifle. "Same plan. We stay here."

Jerry grumbled, shaking his head. "Feels like we're just waiting around, hoping it doesn't pick us next."

Rick sighed, checking the ammo on the table. "It's

frustrating, yeah. But better than running around in the dark and walking straight into it. It just killed three people, after all."

Jerry didn't argue. Instead, he grabbed his coffee and took a slow sip, his expression unreadable.

The scanner continued its occasional bursts of static, each one making them flinch slightly.

After a long pause, Rick set his cup down. "There's something I haven't told you guys before."

Adam and Jerry looked over, interest piqued.

Rick took a deep breath. "About six months ago, we had some... activity at our place."

Jerry leaned in. "What kind of activity?"

Rick hesitated, choosing his words carefully. "We started hearing noises at night. At first, I thought it was just the wind or the usual critters, but it kept happening. Every night, like clockwork."

"You don't think it was the Dogman, do you?" Adam asked, his brow creasing.

Rick shook his head. "No. We think it was a Sasquatch."

Jerry scoffed. "You're serious?"

Rick nodded. "Dead serious. It started with banging on the house, like something was hitting the walls with a massive stick. Then came the screams."

"Screams?" Jerry repeated, voice quieter now.

Rick exhaled. "Yeah. A mix between a siren and a human scream. It was creepy as hell. Like someone dying."

Adam studied him carefully. "You're sure it wasn't just some kids messing around?"

Rick shook his head. "I thought so too, at first. But then things started moving around in the yard. Tools would go missing and turn up in weird places. One morning, I found our rake in a tree, fifteen feet off the ground. No way a kid or the wind did that."

Jerry rubbed his arms as if shaking off a chill. "Were you scared?"

Rick shrugged. "Not exactly scared. Spooked, yeah. Macey was more rattled than me. We thought about calling someone, but it never felt hostile. Just... curious."

Adam nodded. "So what did you do?"

"Nothing much we could do," Rick admitted. "We ignored

it, hoped it would go away. Then, one night, it just… stopped. No more banging, no more screams. Like it never happened."

The room fell into silence. Adam finally spoke. "And you never saw it? Not once?"

Rick shook his head. "Never. Just felt it. Sometimes I'd wake up in the middle of the night, knowing something was watching us. But when I looked outside, nothing was there."

Jerry let out a slow breath. "That's unsettling, man."

Adam nodded. "Well, at least it didn't cause any real harm."

Rick chuckled dryly. "Yeah, we were glad about that.

The anxiety in the room remained, but the conversation had shifted, if only slightly. They had all faced things that defied reason, that most folks would never believe existed.

Adam glanced at the locked doors, his rifle resting beside him. "Alright. Let's focus. We get through tonight, one way or another."

The others nodded. Outside, the wind swept through the trees in uneven bursts, carrying with it the unmistakable scent of something unnatural.

CHAPTER 40

Sheriff Walters drove slowly, his heart heavy with dread. He was on his way to Chief Deputy Turner's house, a task he dreaded more than any other. Informing a loved one of a fallen officer was the hardest part of his job. Tonight, he had to deliver the devastating news to Mark's wife of fifteen years, Karen.

As he pulled up to the modest house, the lights were still on, a sign that Karen was probably still up. The sheriff took a deep breath, steeling himself for what lay ahead. He walked up the front steps and knocked on the door, the sound echoing ominously in the quiet night.

The door opened, and Karen's face lit up with a hopeful smile that quickly faded when she saw the expression on Sheriff Walter's face. "Sheriff? What's wrong? Is it Mark?"

Sheriff Walters took off his hat, holding it in his hands

as he looked into her eyes. "Karen, may I come in?"

She stepped aside, her hands trembling. "Of course. What's happened?"

The sheriff entered the living room, glancing at the family photos on the walls. He had to focus, to find the right words. He turned to Karen, his heart aching. "Karen, there's no easy way to say this. Mark was involved in a serious incident tonight. I'm so sorry... he didn't make it."

Karen's eyes widened in shock, her face going pale. "No... no, that can't be true. Mark can't be gone!"

Sheriff Walters reached out, gently guiding her to sit down on the couch as her legs seemed to give way. "I'm so sorry, Karen. I wish there was more I could say. He was a good man, a great deputy."

Tears streamed down her face as she shook her head, unable to comprehend the words. "H-how did it happen? Wh-what... what happened to him?

The sheriff hesitated, choosing his words carefully. "At this stage, it looks like an animal attack. We're still investigating, and the coroner will call you in the morning with more details."

Karen sobbed, her hands covering her face. "A- an animal

attack? Oh my God, Sheriff. Wa-was this the large wolf everyone was talking about? Mark said it was all a load of bs."

Sheriff Walters knelt beside her, his voice gentle. "It looks like it. Mark... he was doing his job, protecting this community."

Karen nodded through her tears, her body shaking with grief. "I... I don't know what to do. I can't be alone right now."

"Is there someone I can call for you?" Sheriff Walters asked softly. "A friend, family member?"

Karen nodded, her voice barely a whisper. "My sister. She lives close by. Co-could you call her for me?"

"Of course," Sheriff Walters said, taking out his phone. "What's her number?"

Karen gave him the number, and the sheriff quickly dialed it. After a few rings, a concerned voice answered. "Hello?"

"Hi, this is Sheriff Scott Walters. Is this Anna?"

"Yes, it is. Sheriff, what's going on? Is everything alright?"

Sheriff Walters took a deep breath. "Anna, I'm afraid I have some terrible news. There's been an incident, and I'm here with Karen. She needs you right now."

"Oh my God," Anna gasped. "I'll be right there. Please, take care of her until I get there."

"I will," Sheriff Walters assured her. He ended the call and turned back to Karen. "Anna is on her way."

Karen nodded, wiping her eyes. "Thank you, Sheriff. I don't know how I'm going to get through this."

Sheriff Walters placed a comforting hand on her shoulder. "You're not alone, Karen. We're all here for you. Mark was part of our family too, and we're going to do everything we can to support you."

Minutes later Anna rushed in, her face etched with worry. She immediately embraced Karen, who broke down again in her sister's arms. Sheriff Walters stepped back, giving them space.

"I'll be outside if you need anything," he said softly.

As he stood on the porch, the sheriff felt the heavy burden on his shoulders. Mark Turner had been a friend, a colleague, and a dedicated officer. His death was a blow to not only his family, but the entire community.

Anna came out a few minutes later, her eyes red from crying. "Thank you for calling me, Sheriff. I'll take care of her now."

Sheriff Walters nodded. "If you need anything, don't hesitate to call. The department is here for you."

Anna gave a small, grateful smile. "Thank you, Sheriff Walters. We appreciate it."

As the sheriff walked back to his car to head back to the scene, he felt a deep resolve settle within him. He would find the Dogman and put an end to its terror. Mark Turner deserved justice, and Sheriff Walters was determined to see it through.

CHAPTER 41

The taste of blood lingered in the Dogman's mouth, and the adrenaline of the hunt coursed through her veins. She had proven her dominance once more, leaving a trail of destruction in her wake.

The night was quiet now, the only sounds the faint rustling of leaves and the distant hum of the hairless ones moving through their unnatural world. She sniffed the air, her keen senses picking up on every scent and sound. She needed to move quickly, to stay ahead of the response that would inevitably come.

She had taken out the hairless one with the thunderstick and the other two cowering in the metal beast with ruthless efficiency. The attack had been swift and brutal, a testament to her power and cunning. She had relished the fear radiating from them in their final moments. But this was only the beginning.

Her ultimate targets were still out there—the three who had murdered her brother. Their scent was imprinted in her mind, drawing her forward like an unshakable instinct. She would not stop until they lay lifeless beneath her claws.

A dull ache throbbed in her ear where the thunderstick had struck. Blood matted the fur around it, the sting a fresh reminder of the hairless one's pathetic attempt to stop her. It was a minor nuisance, nothing more. The pain only fueled her fury.

She moved swiftly through the town's outskirts, keeping to the shadows. The scent of her prey was strong now. They had been here recently. She prowled silently along the edges of their territory, scanning, waiting.

The Dogman reached a small creek and crouched, lowering her muzzle to the water. She lapped at it, the cool liquid washing away the taste of blood, but doing nothing to dull the fire inside her. Her ears twitched, scanning for movement. She was always aware. Always hunting.

The drink refreshed her, clearing her mind and sharpening her focus. The hairless ones were cunning in their own way, and she knew they would be prepared this time. But she had the advantage, they were afraid. Fear was a powerful weapon, and she wielded it with expert precision.

She rose from the creek and started back toward the town. Her movements were fluid, effortless, the body of a predator honed for the hunt. The scent of the hairless ones' artificial dwellings filled the air. Their glass barriers, their flimsy walls, nothing they built could keep her out.

She approached a particular house, pausing as she recognized the scent. The three were inside. The ones who had stolen her brother's life.

A slow, primal growl rumbled deep in her chest.

But she would not strike yet. The Dogman was patient. She knew the value of waiting, of choosing the perfect moment to attack. She would watch and wait, learn their movements, their weaknesses. When the time was right, she would strike with a fury they could not escape.

She slipped back into the darkness, her glowing eyes never leaving the house. The hunt was on. And soon, she would make them suffer.

CHAPTER 42

Jerry sat in front of the bank of security monitors, his eyes scanning each feed for any sign of movement. The fortified house was surrounded by cameras, each one providing a different angle of the property and the street.

He leaned forward, sipping his coffee, his nerves on edge.

Adam walked into the room, glancing at Jerry. "Anything?"

Jerry shook his head. "Nothing so far. Just a few stray cats and the occasional car driving by. But I'm keeping a close watch."

Rick joined them, looking just as tense. "We're doing the right thing, staying put. But it doesn't make the waiting any easier."

Jerry sighed, rubbing his eyes. "I know. Sitting here is making me go stir crazy."

Adam placed a reassuring hand on Jerry's shoulder. "Me too, brother."

Jerry nodded, appreciating the support. He turned his attention back to the monitors, his eyes darting from one feed to the next. The street outside was quiet, the houses dark and still.

He glanced over at Adam, who was talking quietly with Rick.

Jerry looked back at the monitors, and his heart skipped a beat. There, standing across the road, was the Dogman. Its massive form was partially hidden by the shadows, but its eyes glowed with a vengeful light. It was watching the house, its gaze fixed on the front door.

"Adam! Rick!" Jerry's voice was a harsh whisper, urgent and filled with fear.

Adam and Rick rushed over, their eyes following Jerry's pointing finger to the monitor. The sight of the Dogman sent a chill down their spines.

"Jesus," Rick said. "It's here."

Adam's mind raced. "Stay calm. We've fortified the house, and we're armed. It can't get in without a fight."

Jerry couldn't take his eyes off the screen. The Dogman stood motionless, her eyes never leaving the house. "What's it waiting for?"

Jerry noticed something unusual. The Dogman had pronounced nipples. "It's a female," he said, his voice barely above a whisper.

Adam stared at the monitor, his expression tense. "My gut told me this was connected to us, and I guess I was right. But why me? Was there another one at the cabin that night? And if so, why wait this long for revenge?"

Rick exhaled, shaking his head. "No idea, man. But one thing's for sure, she's here for us."

The question hung in the air.

Minutes felt like hours as Jerry kept his eyes glued to the monitor while Adam and Rick paced the room. The Dogman didn't move, didn't blink. She was a silent, menacing presence, a reminder of the nightmare that had haunted them for so long.

Just as suddenly as she had appeared, the Dogman moved. Her muscular form turned and sprinted away, disappearing into the shadows with a speed that left Jerry breathless. He watched the empty street on the monitor, his heart pounding in his chest.

"Adam, Rick, she's gone!" Jerry called out, his voice shaking.

Adam and Rick hurried back to the monitors, their faces a mix of relief and worry. "What happened?" Adam asked.

"She just took off," Jerry said, pointing at the screen. "One second she was there, and the next she was gone."

Adam's mind raced with possibilities. "She was watching us, trying to intimidate us. But why did she leave?"

"Maybe she's testing us," Jerry suggested. "Seeing how we react, looking for weaknesses."

"Whatever she's doing, we need to stay alert," Adam said. "It knows we're here, and it'll be back."

The three men settled back into their positions, still on alert. The Dogman had made its presence known, a silent threat that loomed over them.

CHAPTER 43

Sheriff Walters had just arrived back at the scene on Whittaker Street. Chaos reigned as the flashing lights of patrol cars bathed the blood-soaked ground in an eerie glow. The sound of radio chatter and hushed conversations filled the air.

Mark's lifeless body lay covered by a white sheet, the brutal reality of the attack hidden from view but not forgotten. The sheriff's gut twisted as he looked at the sheet, knowing that one of his best deputies had fallen victim to a monster that shouldn't exist.

The coroner, Dr. Victoria Purtell, arrived with her assistant, pushing a gurney. Purtell was a seasoned professional, but even she looked shaken by the recent crime scenes. She approached the sheriff, her face a mask of grim determination.

"Sheriff," she greeted, her voice steady despite the tension in the air.

"Victoria," the sheriff replied, nodding. "Thanks for coming so quickly."

Purtell glanced at the covered body. "I'll need to examine the scene and each of the bodies before we move them. This is... beyond words."

Sheriff Walters exhaled, his frustration evident. "It's a horrible mess, isn't it?"

Purtell nodded, turning to her assistant. "Let's get to work. Carefully."

As Purtell and her assistant began their examination, the sheriff's deputies, Davis and Cantrell, worked to secure the area. They set up barriers to keep curious onlookers and potential threats at bay. The local news crews had already started to gather, their cameras capturing every moment.

Sheriff Walter's phone buzzed in his pocket, and he glanced at the caller ID. It was Adam. He stepped away from the chaos to answer.

"Adam, what's going on?" the sheriff asked.

"We saw it, Sheriff," Adam said, his voice tense. He hesitated, then corrected himself. "I mean, *she* was outside my house, watching us. It's a female."

The sheriff's stomach sank. "Are you all okay?"

"Yeah, for now. She left, but we don't know why," Adam said. "We're staying put, but we're ready if she comes back."

"Good," the sheriff said. "Keep your doors locked and stay alert."

"Thanks, Sheriff. Be careful out there," Adam said before hanging up.

Sheriff Walters returned to the scene, the significance of Adam's call sinking in. The Dogman was here for Adam, Rick, and Jerry. That's why she was in town. This wasn't random, it was calculated and personal.

Purtell stood up from where she had been examining Mark's body. She motioned for the sheriff to join her, her face ashen but composed.

"Sheriff, there's no surprises here. These wounds match the other recent cases," Purtell said, her voice steady. "They're deep, precise and extremely effective."

She pointed to the injuries. "Look here. This thing uses its claws just as much as its teeth. It doesn't just slash or rake. It digs in deep and scrapes out."

Sheriff Walters shook his head. "Not your average predator."

Purtell nodded grimly. "Definitely not."

He watched as Purtell and her assistant carefully lifted Mark's body onto the gurney. The scene felt surreal, like something out of a nightmare. But it was all too real, and he had to stay focused.

Davis and Cantrell approached, their expressions grim.

"Sheriff, the media's getting restless," Davis said. "They want a statement."

Sheriff Walters sighed. "Of course they do. Let's go talk to them. We need to control the narrative before it gets out of hand."

He walked over to the makeshift barricade where the reporters were gathered, their cameras and microphones aimed at him. The sheriff took a deep breath, readying himself for the barrage of questions.

"Sheriff Walters, can you tell us what happened here tonight?" one reporter asked, her voice the loudest.

He held up a hand to quiet the crowd. "Ladies and gentlemen, please. We're still in the early stages of our investigation. What I can tell you is that we've had a tragic incident involving one of our deputies and two civilians."

The reporters erupted with questions, but the sheriff continued. "We're working closely with the coroner and other experts to determine exactly what happened. We're taking all necessary precautions to ensure the safety of our community."

"Sheriff, there are rumors of an animal attack. Can you confirm this?" another reporter shouted.

The sheriff paused, choosing his words carefully. "It's likely a wild animal attack, but until I have confirmation from the coroner, I won't be releasing any further details. What I can say is that all residents should remain indoors after dark and take necessary precautions."

"Is there any truth to the rumors about a creature known as the Dogman?" a third reporter asked, pushing forward.

Sheriff Walters' expression remained unreadable. "We've heard those rumors as well. At this time, we have no concrete evidence to support them. Our investigation is ongoing, and we'll provide updates as soon as we have more information."

With that, he turned away from the reporters, not wanting to give them any more fuel for their sensational stories. He motioned for Davis and Cantrell to follow him back to the scene.

As they walked, Cantrell spoke up. "Do you really think it's the Dogman again, Sheriff?"

Sheriff Walters exhaled slowly. "Yes, Cantrell. I am not willing to scare the townspeople or have them not believe us just yet."

They returned to where Purtell was finishing her preliminary examination. She looked up as they approached, her expression somber.

"We're ready to transport the other bodies," she said. "I'll conduct a full autopsy on each first thing in the morning."

"Thank you, Victoria," the sheriff said. "Keep me updated on your findings."

She nodded, and her assistant wheeled the gurneys toward the waiting ambulance. The sheriff watched them go, the burden of responsibility resting heavily on his shoulders. He turned to his deputies.

"Davis, I want you to coordinate with the backup units from here. Make sure they're patrolling the perimeter and keeping an eye out for anything unusual. Cantrell, I need you to stay here and help keep the scene secure until all photos have been taken and all evidence is bagged. We need to gather as much evidence as possible."

"Got it, Sheriff," Davis said, as he got on the radio to organize the patrols.

Cantrell nodded, grabbing her kit and heading toward the crime scene to continue collecting evidence.

Sheriff Walters took a moment to collect his thoughts.

He walked over to his patrol car, leaning against the hood and staring out into the darkness. His mind drifted back to the conversation with Adam. The Dogman had been at his house, watching them. It was a calculated move, meant to intimidate and instil fear.

His phone buzzed again, and he saw it was a message from his wife. She was worried, asking if he was okay. He typed a quick response, assuring her that he was fine but would be working late. He couldn't tell her the full extent of what was happening, not yet. She'd be safer not knowing the details.

He put his phone away and looked around. The scene was a flurry of activity. Officers were taking statements from witnesses, and deputies were combing the area for any clues.

The local fire department had arrived to help illuminate the area with portable floodlights, casting harsh shadows that only added to the night's haunting atmosphere.

CHAPTER 44

Sheriff Walters knew they needed to piece together the events leading up to Mark's death. They needed to understand the pattern, if there was one, and anticipate the Dogman's next move. He walked over to where Cantrell was searching for footprints in a flower bed.

"Any luck?" he asked.

Cantrell shook her head. "Nothing yet, other than the footprints we saw initially."

The sheriff nodded. "Keep at it. Anything you find, no matter how small, could be important."

He turned and saw Davis approaching with a young woman who looked visibly shaken. She had been one of the witnesses, someone who had seen part of the attack from her window. Sheriff Walters walked over to join them.

"Sheriff, this is Claire," Davis said. "She lives just down the street. She saw something but was too scared to come out earlier."

Sheriff Walters offered Claire a reassuring smile. "Claire, thank you for coming forward. Can you tell me what you saw?"

Claire took a deep breath, her eyes wide with fear. "I was getting ready for bed when I heard a commotion outside. At first, I thought it was just some kids messing around, but then I heard a scream. When I looked out my window, I saw... I saw something attacking the officer."

Sheriff Walters nodded, encouraging her to continue. "Can you describe what you saw?"

Claire swallowed hard. "It was much bigger than the officer, like a wolf, but not any wolf I've ever seen. It was dark, covered in fur, and it moved so fast. I could see its eyes—they were glowing an orangey amber color, and it had these huge claws. It was a Werewolf, Sheriff."

Sheriff Walter's blood ran cold. "Thank you, Claire. You've been very helpful. If you remember anything else, please let us know."

Claire nodded, her hands shaking. "Do you think it's still out there?"

The sheriff hesitated, choosing his words carefully. "We're doing everything we can to find it and keep everyone safe. Stay inside, lock your doors, and don't hesitate to call if you see anything unusual."

As Claire walked away, the sheriff turned to Davis. "We need to remind the patrols of what they should be looking for. But I don't want any word of it reaching the public, just yet."

Davis nodded, taking out his radio. "I'll make sure everyone's reminded."

Sheriff Walters took another deep breath as he walked back to his patrol car.

The hunt for the Dogman was on, and Sheriff Walters was determined to bring it to an end. For Mark, for the road workers, and the other victims. The Dogman was elusive, but their resolve was stronger.

CHAPTER 45

Sheriff Walters' frustration boiled beneath the surface as he grabbed his phone and dialed the FBI. He was exhausted, fed up with their runaround, and furious that their delays were costing lives. Carlisle had one attack, but Hickory had been under siege for days with no FBI in sight. Something had to change.

The phone rang a few times before a voice answered. "Special Agent Johnson speaking."

"Special Agent Johnson, this is Sheriff Walters from Hickory," he began, his voice taut with barely suppressed rage. "We've got a serious problem here, and I need to know why your team isn't back here already."

There was a brief pause before Special Agent Johnson replied. "Sheriff Walters, I understand your frustration, but the decision to deploy our team again is above my pay grade.

We're doing what we can."

Sheriff Walters shook his head. "Doing what you can? My Chief Deputy is dead because of this... thing! We needed your help yesterday, not sometime in the future when it's convenient for you."

"Sheriff, I get it," Johnson said, his tone growing defensive. "But I don't make the decisions. The orders come from higher up, and they're cautious about how they handle situations like this."

"Cautious? Is that what you call it?" Sheriff Walters' voice rose with anger. "We've had multiple attacks, people are dead, and now one of my own men has been killed. How many more people must die before your superiors decide to take action?"

Johnson sighed. "Sheriff, you must understand. When it comes to incidents involving potential cryptids or unexplained phenomena, the bureaucratic wheels turn slowly. There are protocols, clearances, and..."

Sheriff Walters cut him off. "Protocols? Clearances? This isn't some paper-pushing exercise, Johnson. This is real. People are dying. We're doing everything we can here, but we need your resources, your expertise. If your team had been here when we first called, maybe Mark would still be alive. You attended the massacre in Carlisle. Why aren't we receiving the proper support?"

"I'm sorry for your loss, Sheriff," Johnson said, his voice softening slightly. "But the reality is, my hands are tied. I've been pushing for immediate action, but I'm hitting walls. The best I can do is keep pressing and hope they'll send reinforcements sooner rather than later."

The sheriff took a deep breath, trying to control his fury. "We don't have time for 'sooner rather than later,' Special Agent Johnson. We need action now. I need your team here, on the ground, ready to help us deal with this threat. If you can't make that happen, then get me someone who can. The media are already asking questions. It won't take long for this to go nationwide."

"I'll do what I can, Sheriff," Johnson replied, his tone firm. "I'll escalate this and push harder. But I need you to keep your people safe in the meantime. Don't engage unless absolutely necessary."

Sheriff Walters rubbed his jaw. "We don't have the luxury of avoiding engagement, Johnson. This thing is hunting people in town. We're not just going to sit around and wait for it to pick us off one by one."

"I understand, Sheriff," Johnson said. "I'll get back to you as soon as I have an update. And I promise, I'll do everything in my power to expedite this."

"Make sure you do," the sheriff said before hanging up, his frustration boiling over. He stared at the phone in his hand, feeling helpless and angry.

CHAPTER 46

The Sheriff paced back and forth outside his cruiser. The grim events of the night demanded swift and decisive action. He couldn't wait for the FBI to get their act together. They needed to act now. He spotted Cantrell and Davis near the wrecked cruiser and called them over.

"We need to set up a command center at the town hall. We can't afford to wait any longer," Sheriff Walters said, his voice firm and determined.

Cantrell nodded, her expression resolute. "You're right, Sheriff. We need to coordinate our efforts and keep the town better informed."

Davis glanced around at the chaotic scene, then back at the sheriff. "What's the plan?"

Sheriff Walters took a deep breath, steadying himself.

"First, we need to reinforce our warnings to the townsfolk. Let them know how serious this is. We can't have any more casualties."

Cantrell's eyes widened slightly, but she quickly regained her composure. "You don't want to mention the Dogman?"

"The higher-ups would have a field day if we admitted the Dogman was real," the sheriff said, shaking his head. "Besides, some of the townsfolk wouldn't take it seriously, and it would put more people at risk. Our deputies can know the truth, but we can't tell the general public."

Cantrell nodded in agreement. "Fair enough, Sheriff.

Looking at Cantrell the sheriff continued. "I'll need you to handle the logistics of setting up the command center. Get the necessary equipment and personnel to the town hall as quickly as possible," Sheriff Walters directed.

Cantrell nodded, already making mental notes. "I'll get on it right away, Sheriff."

The sheriff turned to Davis, his tone resolute. "Davis, I need you to step into Mark's role today and take charge of organizing patrols. We need a structured response, and you're the one to make sure it happens. First, ensure every deputy understands exactly what they're looking for. This thing is calculated and lethal. Pair them up, no one goes out alone under any circumstances." He fixed Davis with a steady look. "Make sure every deputy has their rifles on them at all times when they're outside their patrol cars. Radios and flashlights, no exceptions."

He let that sink in before continuing. "And one more thing, do not tell the public that we believe this is a Dogman. We can't have people panicking or forming their own hunting parties. That will just create more victims. Keep it controlled. During the day, keep patrols routine and keep people calm. But when night falls, I want double the patrols and I want every off-duty deputy and reserve called in. We need as eyes in town as possible."

"Got it, Sheriff. I'll coordinate with the others and set up a detailed schedule for the next couple of days," Davis replied.

The sheriff cast a look at the morning sky. "We need everything in place before nightfall. I know your shifts are almost up, but get started now please, then take some time to rest. Let's move fast."

The three of them dispersed, each heading to their respective tasks.

Sheriff Walters made his way to his cruiser and grabbed the radio. "Dispatch, this is Sheriff Walters. We're setting up a command center at the town hall. Inform all units to report there before their shifts for a briefing."

The dispatcher's voice crackled through the radio.

"Copy that, Sheriff. All units will be notified."

The sheriff called Adam on his phone. "Adam, we're setting up a command center at the town hall. I need you, Jerry, and Rick to get some shut-eye and head into the center as soon as you can. Make sure you all stay together and bring your guns to stay safe."

"We'll be there, sheriff. Thanks for the heads-up," Adam replied.

CHAPTER 47

At 6 a.m., Sheriff Walters headed toward town hall, his mind running through plans and contingencies. Fatigue settled deep in his bones after days of little sleep, and for once, he gave in, pulling into a drive-thru for a strong coffee. He rarely stopped for one, but after the past week, he needed it.

By the time he arrived, town hall was already alive with movement. Officials and emergency personnel had begun to gather, drawn by the urgency of the situation.

Inside the main hall, Cantrell was directing the setup of tables, communication equipment, and maps of the area.

She looked up as the sheriff entered. "We're almost ready, Sheriff. I've got the comms team setting up a central hub here. We'll be able to coordinate everything from this room."

"Good work, Cantrell," Sheriff Walters said, appreciating

her efficiency. He moved to the front of the room and called for attention. "Listen up, everyone. We're dealing with a critical situation. As you may know, there's a large, dangerous animal on the loose. Until further notice, we need to enforce a curfew from sunset to dawn. If people must be out, they should go in pairs only. Our priority is to protect the public and track down this threat."

The impact of his statement was clear as heads nodded in agreement.

"Davis, how are the patrols coming?" Sheriff Walters asked.

Davis stepped forward. "We've got teams ready to go at sunset. They'll be patrolling in pairs, fully equipped."

"Excellent. Make sure they stay in constant contact. If anyone sees anything, they report it immediately and do not engage alone," Sheriff Walters ordered.

He turned back to the assembled team. "We need to get the word out now. Radio, social media, emergency alerts, everything. People need to know about the curfew. Let's move quickly and efficiently."

Cantrell was on her phone, coordinating with the local radio station to broadcast a warning. Meanwhile, Davis contacted the sheriff's office administration, instructing them to post an advisory on social media, urging residents to stay indoors after dusk.

CHAPTER 48

By midday, the town hall was a flurry of activity. Its large meeting rooms and access to communication equipment made it the perfect choice for coordinating their efforts. Tables were set up with maps, radios, and laptops.

Deputies and volunteers moved with purpose, each one understanding the gravity of the situation. Sheriff Walters stood at the center, overseeing the setup and ensuring everything was in place.

"Davis, make sure we have direct lines to all patrol units," Sheriff Walters instructed. "We need constant communication. No blackouts."

"Got it, Sheriff," Davis replied, walking to the communication hub.

Sheriff Walters turned to Cantrell. "From nightfall, I will

want updates every hour on patrol movements and any sightings. We can't afford to miss anything."

"Understood, Sheriff," Cantrell said, jotting down notes.

A few minutes later, Adam, Jerry, and Rick arrived at the town hall. They were greeted by a flurry of activity but were quickly directed to the central meeting room where the sheriff was waiting.

"Thanks for coming," the sheriff said, shaking their hands. "We need all the help we can get. You've faced this thing before, and we need your insights."

Adam nodded. "We'll do whatever we can to help."

Jerry and Rick echoed Adam's sentiment, their faces grim with determination. They gathered around the main table, where Sheriff Walters had laid out maps of the town and surrounding areas.

"We've set up patrols and checkpoints here," Sheriff Walters explained, pointing to various locations on the map. "But we're spread thin. We need to figure out its pattern, its movements. Anything you can tell us will help."

Adam leaned over the map, running his finger along the marked locations. "I went over the reports again last night," he said, eyes narrowed in concentration. "Based on the attack sites, I'd bet it's coming from this direction." He pointed to a stretch of land on the map. "It's been striking around Whittaker Street, but I think it's holed up here." He circled an area further out. "This is probably where it's hiding during the day."

Jerry leaned in, studying the map. "That's a big area, but this thing can cover ground fast. Ten, twenty miles a night is nothing to it. As long as it has a water source and prey, it'll keep moving."

The sheriff nodded. "Makes sense. But I don't want to send out search parties just yet. That's a good way to get more people killed. No one around here is prepared to hunt a predator like this."

Adam tapped the map. "What about setting up a checkpoint at the end of Whittaker Street? If it comes through there again, we might be able to track it."

"Good idea," the sheriff agreed. "I'll make sure a unit is stationed there tonight."

Rick exhaled sharply. "Doesn't matter how we play this, it's going to come for us, eventually. But anyone who crosses its path is in just as much danger. Hell, for all we know, it could come here."

Adam glanced out into the main room, where deputies and volunteers moved with urgency. "We're locked and loaded, and a lot of others are too," he said.

Sheriff Walters nodded, absorbing their input. "We've increased patrols and are keeping a close watch on the hot spots, but we need to be ready for anything. What about traps? Could we lure it into a controlled area?"

Adam considered the idea. "It's possible, but risky. It's strong and smart. If we set a trap, it has to be foolproof."

Jerry shook his head. "I doubt this town has anything that could hold something that size."

"We'll work on that," the sheriff said. "In the meantime, I want you all to stay here and help coordinate. I know you're itching to get out there and take this thing down, and I can't force you to stay. But think of your families. It's safer here, and your experience is invaluable."

Adam exchanged glances with Jerry and Rick before nodding. "As much as we'd like to be the ones to take it down, you're right, Sheriff. It's best we stay put and help from here. You can count on us to stay out of the way and do what needs to be done."

"Good," the sheriff said with a firm nod.

With that, they all rose from their seats and stepped back into the controlled chaos of the main room, ready to do their part.

CHAPTER 49

In the control center, as Sheriff Walters reviewed strategies with his deputies, the phone rang, displaying a blocked number. His gut told him it was the FBI. He stepped away from the table, exhaling sharply before answering.

"Sheriff Walters," he said, trying to keep his voice steady.

"Sheriff, this is FBI Senior Special Agent Don Edwards, Special Agent Johnson's supervisor. I've been briefed on your situation."

Sheriff Walters felt a glimmer of hope. "Senior Special Agent Edwards, thank you for calling. We need your team here urgently. This situation is escalating."

"I understand, Sheriff," Edwards replied. "We're mobilizing a team as we speak, but there are logistical challenges."

"Logistical challenges?" Sheriff Walters echoed, his frustration bubbling up again. "People are dying, Senior Special Agent Edwards. We don't have time for logistics. We need action."

Edwards sighed. "I know, Sheriff. Believe me, I'm doing everything I can to expedite this. But we're dealing with a high-level threat that requires careful handling. We can't afford to make mistakes."

Sheriff Walters clenched his fist. "We can't afford more deaths, Senior Special Agent Edwards. I've already lost a deputy last night. He had a family. My people are terrified. We need your help now."

There was a brief pause on the line. "We're on our way, Sheriff. Hang tight. And in the meantime, do everything you can to keep your community safe. We'll be there before nightfall."

Sheriff Walters ended the call, feeling a mixture of relief and anger. The FBI was coming, but he knew it was already too late for some. He re-entered the command center, where the atmosphere was buzzing.

"Listen up, everyone," Sheriff Walters called out, getting

the attention of the room. "The FBI is finally sending a team, but we need to hold the line until they get here. Double-check your equipment, stay in constant communication, and look out for each other. We're in this together."

The deputies and volunteers nodded, their expressions resolute. Sheriff Walters moved over to the radio operator. "Any updates from the patrols?"

The operator shook his head. "Nothing significant yet, Sheriff. Just a few false alarms. As you said, it probably sleeps during the day."

Sheriff Walters nodded. "Keep me posted."

CHAPTER 50

As Adam, Jerry, and Rick continued brainstorming strategies to capture or kill the Dogman, Sheriff Walters overheard their discussion. He stepped closer, crossing his arms as he listened, then finally spoke.

"You're thinking ahead. That's good," he said, his tone measured. "We need to be proactive, not just wait for this thing to strike again."

"We need to consider bait," Sheriff Walters said. "But as we discussed, it has to be safe for whoever is involved. How can we lure this thing out without putting someone in harm's way?"

Adam thought for a moment. "We could use remote technology. Set up sound decoys or even scent lures that could attract it to a specific location."

Jerry nodded. "And we could reinforce that area with traps. Not just conventional ones, but something stronger, more resilient."

Rick added, "If we can funnel it into a controlled environment, we might have a better chance. Focus on the area on the border of town where Adam suggested it comes from."

Sheriff Walters nodded in agreement. "Alright, let's start setting this up. Davis, coordinate with the tech team to get the scent lures set up in the right places. Remember, anyone who goes out must go in pairs. No one goes alone. Cantrell, keep monitoring any new reports or sightings. I doubt there will be any during the daylight hours, but you never know."

The team worked tirelessly throughout the day, setting up scent lures. They mapped out a strategy that combined technology with manpower, using the resources at their disposal to create a fortified perimeter around the town.

CHAPTER 51

It was 1pm in Hickory when members of the public began to converge on the command center. News had spread rapidly through the small town, fueled by whispers and rumors of a creature terrorizing the area, a creature many were calling the Dogman.

The command center, a usually quiet municipal building, was now the epicenter of curiosity and concern. A crowd gathered outside, voices growing louder and more insistent as the minutes passed. Among them were families worried about their children, business owners concerned about the safety of their establishments, and individuals who had lost loved ones in the recent attacks.

Inside the command center, Sheriff Walters and his deputies exchanged anxious glances. They had anticipated public concern, but the sheer number of people now demanding answers was overwhelming. Adam, Jerry, and Rick stood nearby, watching the commotion unfold on the monitors.

"I need to address this," Sheriff Walters said, his voice steady despite the anxiety etched on his face.

Deputy Davis nodded. "I'll support you. We need to keep control of the situation."

Sheriff Walters stepped outside, followed by Deputy Davis, Adam, Jerry, and Rick. The crowd immediately erupted in questions and demands for information.

"Is it true? Is there really a Dogman?" a woman in the front called out.

"What are you doing to keep us safe?" another voice demanded.

"Is a Dogman a werewolf, Sheriff?" someone else asked.

The sheriff raised his hands, signaling for silence. "Please, everyone, calm down. I understand your concerns, and we're here to provide some answers."

Sheriff Walters took a deep breath. "Yes, there have been reports of a dangerous creature in the area. We are taking these reports very seriously and are doing everything in our power to ensure the safety of the town."

The crowd murmured with skepticism. One man, standing near the front, stepped forward. He was tall, with a stern face and an air of arrogance.

"That's all well and good, Sheriff, but what about the people who have already been killed?" he demanded, his voice loud and accusatory. "What are you going to do to make sure this doesn't happen again?"

The man's relentless questioning drew the attention of everyone around him. "And how do we know there aren't more of these things out there? My brother was killed by that monster, and I want to know what you're doing to protect us! Closing our doors at night isn't going to stop this abomination!"

The sheriff met the man's gaze. "I'm deeply sorry for your loss. I can't imagine the pain you're going through. We've increased patrols, we're working closely with federal agencies, and we have the resources in place to handle any further threats."

The man wasn't satisfied. "Words won't bring back my brother, Sheriff. We need action, not promises. How can you guarantee our safety?"

Sheriff Walters stepped forward. "We're taking this situation very seriously. But we need your cooperation. Everyone should stay indoors after dusk and report any suspicious activity immediately. If you have weapons, I suggest to you keep them handy, but safely secured."

Despite the reassurances, the crowd remained on edge. Whispers and murmurs of fear and doubt rippled through the assembly. The man continued to push, his voice rising above the others.

"That's not good enough! How do we know you're not hiding something from us? How many more have to die before you get this under control?"

Jerry stepped forward, unable to stay silent any longer. "We understand your frustration, but attacking the people who are trying to help won't solve anything. We're all in this together, and we need to work as a community to stay safe."

The man's face flushed with anger. "Easy for you to say, jackass! You weren't out there when my brother was torn apart. All we've got to bury is pieces of him!"

Sheriff Walters raised his hands again. "Enough! We understand you're scared, but we need to stay calm and focused. We are all doing everything we can to keep this town safe. We need to trust each other and work together."

A woman in the crowd, holding her young child close, spoke up. "What should we do to protect our families, Sheriff?"

"Stay indoors from sunset to sunrise," Walters replied. "If you have to go out, travel in groups. Report anything unusual immediately. If you have firearms, keep them nearby. We're setting up a hotline for tips and information. We need everyone to be our eyes and ears."

Adam, seeing the tension ease slightly, added, "We've seen how strong this community can be. When we work together, we can overcome anything. Let's support each other."

The crowd began to murmur in agreement, the initial anger and fear giving way to a cautious resolve. The arrogant man, though still visibly upset, seemed to accept the reality of the situation. He stepped back, his shoulders slumping slightly.

The sheriff took the opportunity to reinforce their message. "We're not alone in this. We have the resources, the expertise, and the community strength to handle this threat. We need your help to keep everyone safe. We're in this together, and together, we'll get through it. If you have questions or need support, we're here for you. Let's stay united and strong."

The crowd began to disperse, reassured by the commitment and resolve of their leaders. Families gathered their children, friends comforted each other, and the town of Hickory slowly returned to a semblance of normalcy.

Back inside the command center, Sheriff Walters, Deputy Davis, Adam, Jerry, and Rick took a moment to reflect on the encounter.

"That was intense," Rick said, exhaling deeply.

Sheriff Walters nodded. "People are scared. We need to keep that in mind and do everything we can to reassure them."

Adam added, "And we need to keep working together, just like we told them."

Rick agreed. "We have a lot of work ahead of us, but we've made progress. Let's stay focused and keep pushing forward."

CHAPTER 52

It was just after 3.30pm when the FBI team arrived at the town hall. Senior Special Agent Edwards and Special Agent Johnson led a group of agents into the command center, their presence bringing a sense of relief but also heightening the urgency of the situation.

"Sheriff Walters," Edwards said, shaking the sheriff's hand. "We're here to help."

"About time," Sheriff Walters replied, his tone more relieved than accusatory. "We've set up a command center and have been coordinating patrols and traps. We could use your expertise."

Edwards glanced around. "We've reviewed the reports and have some additional equipment that might help. Thermal imaging, motion sensors, anything to give us an edge. We also brought a specialized trap designed to capture the Dogman. If we can lure it into a specific area, we'll deploy the trap, shoot it with tranquilizer darts, and load it into the back of the FBI truck."

The sheriff nodded, grateful for the support. "We'll take anything you've got. This is not your average animal."

The FBI agents quickly integrated into the command center, setting up their equipment and sharing their knowledge. The collaboration between local law enforcement and the federal agents brought a renewed sense of hope.

Senior Special Agent Edwards called for a briefing, gathering everyone around the central table. "Alright, everyone. We've dealt with similar cases before, but this one is different. The key is understanding this creature's behavior—it's not just an animal, but a predator with intelligence and strategy. Special Agents will remain here in the Command Center to coordinate and monitor, while our field team will be stationed near the trap. They'll be in position by nightfall. Special Agent Johnson will lead the operation, and I'll be overseeing it."

Johnson added, "We'll be using thermal imaging to track its movements when it gets dark. In the meantime, my team will install sensors around the areas it has frequented before, with the trap at the center. If the Dogman appears, the sensors will go off."

The sheriff turned to Davis. "Davis, coordinate with the FBI on where your team have placed the scent lures."

Davis nodded. "Got it, Sheriff."

Sheriff Walters continued, "Cantrell, keep monitoring any new reports or sightings. We need to stay on top of this and respond immediately to any new information."

Cantrell nodded, already checking her equipment. "I'm on it, Sheriff."

As the preparations continued, the atmosphere in the command center grew more focused. Everyone knew that the real test was yet to come. They were buying time, reinforcing their defenses, and gathering every possible advantage before the Dogman struck again.

Special Agents Johnson, Miller, Richardson, and Hernandez coordinated with the local deputies, sharing information and strategizing their next moves. The collaboration was seamless, a testament to the professionalism and dedication of both the local law enforcement and the federal agents.

The integration of the FBI's technology was a game-changer. The drones, in particular, provided a significant advantage. Equipped with infrared cameras and heat sensors, they could detect movement and body heat even in the dense forest that surrounded Hickory. This allowed the team to monitor a vast area without having to send out patrols, reducing the risk to personnel.

In the command center, Special Agent Miller sat at a console, managing the sensor feed. Special Agents Richardson and Hernandez placed the sensors at the Dogman hotspots, ensuring all sensors were online once installed.

Sheriff Walters and Special Agent Johnson stood nearby, discussing their strategy. "We need to be proactive," Walters said, his voice resolute. "If we wait for it to come to us, more people could get hurt. We need to find it and neutralize the threat."

Johnson agreed. "We'll continue to monitor the feeds and coordinate our ground units. The drones will give us the advantage, but we need to be ready to move at a moment's notice."

As the sun began to set, the unease in the command center continued to build. The special agents and deputies knew that any moment could bring the breakthrough they were waiting for.

In the logistics area, Deputy Jesse Rodriguez coordinated the supply chain, ensuring that the team had everything they needed. "We've got more ammo coming in, as well as additional medical supplies," he reported to Sheriff Walters. "We're also setting up a rest area for the team, cots, food, water. We need to be prepared for a long night."

Walters nodded. "Good work, Rodriguez. Make sure everyone stays hydrated and takes breaks when they can. We need everyone at their best."

Outside, the town of Hickory was unnervingly quiet.

The usual sounds of the evening, dogs barking, children playing, and cars driving by, were absent. Instead, an oppressive silence hung in the air.

Special Agent Johnson addressed the team once more. "Remember, the key is to lure the Dogman into the area with the trap. When it shows up, we'll deploy the trap, shoot it with tranquilizer darts, and secure it in the FBI truck. Stay focused and be ready to act at a moment's notice."

The sheriff nodded, his determination mirrored in the faces around him. "Alright, let's get to work. We're hunting a predator tonight, and we need to be ready for anything."

CHAPTER 53

Special Agent Johnson gathered everyone around a large table in the command center. On it was a detailed blueprint of the FBI's sophisticated trap, a device that had been successfully used in other high-profile captures. The room was filled with local deputies, FBI special agents, and town officials, all eager to understand the plan. Just outside of town, a specialized FBI unit was already at the designated site, ensuring the trap was in place and functioning as intended.

"Alright, everyone," Johnson began, pointing to the blueprint. "This is our primary tool for capturing the Dogman. It's a specialized containment system designed to secure large, intelligent predators. We've deployed it successfully in previous cases, and we're confident it will work here."

Senior Special Agent Edwards stepped forward, holding a

remote. "The setup includes a reinforced steel cage engineered to withstand significant force. It's camouflaged to blend in with the environment, reducing the chance of the creature detecting it before stepping inside."

Johnson continued, "The trap is baited with scent lures designed to mimic the scent of its prey. These lures are strategically placed to draw the Dogman toward the enclosure."

Edwards clicked a button on the remote, and a 3D model of the trap appeared on a large screen. "Once the Dogman steps inside, motion sensors trigger the doors to close. These doors are nearly silent, ensuring the creature isn't startled before the mechanism is fully engaged."

Sheriff Walters studied the screen. "What about sedation? How do we keep it from fighting back?"

Edwards smiled. "That's where phase two of containment comes in. The trap is equipped with automated tranquilizer dart systems. Once the doors lock, the system deploys a fast-acting sedative that will put the Dogman under within seconds."

Special Agent Miller, who was managing the sensor feed, spoke up. "We've also integrated a remote monitoring system. We'll be able to track the Dogman's movements in real-time and ensure we know when it's approaching the site."

Johnson pointed to the areas surrounding the trap. "Motion sensors and thermal imaging cameras are in place around the perimeter. These will alert us to any movement and help guide the Dogman in."

Sheriff Walters nodded, feeling a cautious sense of optimism. "And once it's secured?"

Edwards answered, "Once sedated, it will be transferred into the reinforced transport cage inside our specialized truck. The vehicle is designed for high-risk containment, ensuring no chance of escape during transport."

Adam, Jerry, and Rick, who had been listening intently, exchanged glances. Adam spoke up, "This all sounds solid, but what if it doesn't go according to plan? What's the fallback?"

Johnson nodded. "Good question. If the trap fails or the Dogman avoids it, our backup teams will engage with tranquilizer guns. We have ground units stationed near the site, ready to intervene if necessary. The key is working together and maintaining constant communication."

Sheriff Walters turned to the deputies in the room. "I want everyone to follow the plan exactly. We stay vigilant, we stay coordinated, and we don't take unnecessary risks."

Special Agent Miller stepped forward, his expression serious. "It's time to launch aerial surveillance. The drones will give us a wide-area view and real-time updates on any movement."

Sheriff Walters agreed. "Get them in the air. Keep me updated on anything unusual."

The team dispersed, each member acutely aware of the stakes. The trap was set, the technology was in place, and now they waited.

Miller and his team quickly launched the drones, ensuring they were equipped with infrared cameras and heat sensors. As the drones took off, the screens in the command center came alive with aerial views of the surrounding forest and town, highlighting potential threats.

"Drones are active," Miller reported. "We have full coverage over the area."

Sheriff Walters watched the feeds, the atmosphere in the room heightened. "Good. Now let's see if this thing takes the bait."

CHAPTER 54

As preparations continued, Deputy Rodriguez approached Sheriff Walters with a look of concern. "Sheriff, we've got a situation," he said, glancing at the activity in the command center.

"What is it, Rodriguez?" the sheriff asked, his attention immediately focused.

"One of the patrols just reported seeing about six RVs heading through town, likely going to the RV campground on the outskirts," Rodriguez explained. "One of them had the signage *Dukes of Cryptids* on the side."

The sheriff exhaled sharply, rubbing his temples. "Who the hell are these guys?"

Rodriguez sighed. "Some online group. A bunch of so-called cryptid hunters who post their investigations on

YouTube."

Sheriff Walters frowned. "You're telling me we've got amateur thrill-seekers running around when we're dealing with a real threat?"

"Looks that way," Rodriguez said. "My guess is they're here hoping to catch footage of the Dogman."

Special Agent Johnson, overhearing the exchange, walked over with a scowl. "Great. That's just what we need. Some clueless wannabes stumbling into the middle of an active operation. They could get themselves or worse, one of our team killed."

Sheriff Walters nodded, frustration clear on his face. "We need to head them off before they get themselves into trouble. Rodriguez, get a couple of deputies and go to the RV campground. Tell them they need to stay put and out of the way. Make it very clear this isn't a game."

"On it, Sheriff," Rodriguez replied, turning to leave.

As Rodriguez headed out, Johnson turned to the sheriff. "We should also keep an eye on them. If they're determined to go out looking for the Dogman, they could end up complicating our efforts."

"I agree," Sheriff Walters said. "I'll have one of our patrols keep tabs on them, discreetly. We don't want them wandering into the trap or getting in the way of our teams."

****

As night fell, Deputy Rodriguez, along with Deputies Davis and Cantrell, arrived at the RV campground. The RVs were parked in a semi-circle, and a group of people were setting up cameras and equipment.

"Excuse me," Rodriguez called out, approaching the group. "I'm Deputy Rodriguez with the Hickory Sheriff's Department. We need to talk."

A man in his mid-thirties, wearing a *"Dukes of Cryptids"* T-shirt, stepped forward. "Hey there, Deputy. I'm Derek and we're the *Dukes of Cryptids*. We're here to document the Dogman. This is gonna be great for our channel."

Rodriguez raised his hand. "I understand you're here for your YouTube channel, but this isn't a safe situation. There's a large, dangerous animal loose, and we have a coordinated effort to capture it. You need to stay here and not interfere."

"But we've got experience with this stuff," the man insisted. "We've caught footage of Bigfoot, Chupacabra, and more. We know what we're doing."

Rodriguez shook his head. "I'm sure you've had some

interesting experiences, but this is different. This creature has already caused casualties. We don't want any more people getting hurt. On top of that, the FBI has an ongoing operation out here, and you don't want to catch their eye. Stay here, and let the professionals handle it."

The man looked like he wanted to argue, but then he saw the seriousness in Rodriguez's eyes. "Alright, Deputy. We'll stay here. But if you need any help, we're ready."

Rodriguez nodded. "Thank you. Please understand, this isn't about keeping you from your work. It's about keeping everyone safe."

As Rodriguez and his deputies headed back to their patrol cars, he radioed back to the command center. "Sheriff, we've spoken with the *Dukes of Cryptids*. They've agreed to stay at the campground, but I've got a feeling they might try to sneak out anyway. I've assigned a patrol to keep an eye on them."

"Good work, Rodriguez," Sheriff Walters replied. "Let's hope they stay put. We've got enough to worry about without dealing with thrill-seekers getting in the way."

The Dukes of Cryptids were huddled around a campfire, discussing their plan. "We need to find a way to get closer to the action," one of them said. "This is a once-in-a-lifetime opportunity."

Derek looked thoughtful. "We promised the deputy we'd stay put. But maybe we can set up some cameras in the nearby woods, just to see what's going on."

They nodded in agreement, oblivious to the danger they were putting themselves in.

CHAPTER 55

The town was quiet, its residents locked up tight for the night, likely having dinner or watching TV, unaware of the operation unfolding beyond their walls. Special Agent Miller and his team had deployed the drones, their advanced technology providing a crucial advantage in the hunt for the Dogman. Each drone was equipped with infrared cameras and heat sensors, capable of detecting even the slightest movement in the night.

Miller stood at a console, his eyes fixed on the multiple screens displaying live feeds from the drones. "Alright, we've got drones covering the entire perimeter of the town and the surrounding forest. This will give us a comprehensive view and help us track any movement."

The drones operated with a quiet hum, their rotors barely audible as they hovered over Hickory and its outskirts. They moved in a coordinated pattern, ensuring no area was left unmonitored. The infrared cameras painted a vivid picture of the landscape below, highlighting heat signatures that stood out against the cool night air.

"Drones One and Two are covering the forest to the north and east," Miller said, narrating the positions to the team. "Drones Three and Four are focused on the town itself, and Drones Five and Six are monitoring south and west, including the RV campground."

Sheriff Walters, standing beside Special Agent Johnson, watched the feeds intently. "This technology is impressive. We should be able to catch any movement long before it gets close."

Johnson nodded. "The drones give us the eyes we need. We just have to act quickly."

Every team member was on high alert, knowing that the slightest sign of movement could mean the Dogman was near. Minutes turned into hours, and the screens showed nothing but the usual nocturnal activity of small animals and the occasional.

Suddenly, one of the drones began to beep. Miller's eyes snapped to the screen. "We've got movement on Drone Four. Heat signature detected."

The room came alive with a flurry of activity as everyone focused on the feed from Drone Four. The infrared camera highlighted a large, moving figure against the backdrop of the forest.

"Zoom in," Johnson ordered.

Miller complied, the camera zooming in on the figure.

The image became clearer, revealing a massive figure moving through the landscape. Its sheer size and the way it moved left little doubt this had to be the Dogman. It navigated the terrain with calculated fluidity, its powerful form highlighted in the infrared feed.

"That's it," Sheriff Walters said, his voice tense. "Where is this?" Miller checked the coordinates on the screen. "It's heading southwest, moving towards the RV campground."

Sheriff Walters' heart sank. "Damn it. Those cryptid hunters are right in its path. We need to move fast."

The sheriff grabbed his radio. "All units near the campground, be advised. The Dogman has been spotted heading in your direction. Stay alert, secure the area, and report any movement immediately."

The deputies sprang into action, coordinating their efforts to converge on the campground, while the FBI team hiding near the trap stayed where they were, ready to act if the Dogman changed its course. The drones continued to track the Dogman's movements, providing real-time updates to the team on the ground.

"Keep the drones on it," Sheriff Walters instructed. "We need to know exactly where it's going."

"Drone Four will maintain visual," Miller directed. "Drones Three and Five will spread out and cover the surrounding area."

The infrared feed showed the Dogman moving swiftly through the trees, its path unerringly directed towards the RV campground. The cryptid hunters were oblivious to the danger.

"It's getting too damn close," Miller said, pointing to the screen. "It's almost at the edge of the campground."

Sheriff Walters turned to Davis. "Get in touch with your patrol out there. Make sure they get the tourists inside their campers immediately. No one stays outside."

"I'm on it", Davis said.

CHAPTER 56

Anticipation hung in the still, pine-scented air of the RV campground. The Dukes of Cryptids members huddled around their campfire, unaware of the impending danger. They were equipped with cameras, night vision goggles, shotguns, and 9mm pistols, ready to venture into the woods in search of the elusive Dogman.

"Alright, team, this is our chance to capture the Dogman on film," said Derek, the group's leader. He was a tall, confident man with a bushy beard and an air of arrogance that masked his inexperience. "We've got all the gear we need, and tonight's the night we make history."

"Got the cameras ready?" asked Griffin, another member of the group. He was shorter and stockier, with a nervous energy that contrasted sharply with Derek's bravado.

"Yeah, they're all set," replied Sarah, the tech expert of the group. She adjusted her night vision goggles and checked the batteries in her camera. "We'll get some great footage tonight."

"Remember, stick together and stay quiet," Derek instructed. "We don't want to spook it before we get some solid evidence."

The group of nine gathered their gear, their excitement growing as they prepared to leave the relative safety of the campground. They moved in a tight formation, their flashlights piercing the darkness as they ventured into the woods. The night vision goggles illuminated the path ahead, casting a haunting green glow over the forest.

"Keep your eyes peeled," Derek whispered. "We don't know where it might be hiding."

As they moved through the forest, the night sounds sharpened. Branches creaked in the breeze, the distant, haunting call of a Chuck-will's-widow echoed, and the occasional snap of a twig underfoot broke the stillness. A charged unease settled over the group, each member hyper-aware of their surroundings.

Suddenly, a low growl broke the silence. The group froze, their flashlights darting around to find the source of the sound.

"What was that?" Griffin asked, his voice trembling.

"I don't know," Derek replied, trying to keep his voice steady. "Just stay calm and keep moving."

Another growl, this time closer. The hairs on the back of their necks stood up as they realized they were not alone.

"There!" Sarah pointed towards a pair of glowing eyes reflecting the light from their flashlights. The Dogman emerged from the shadows, its huge frame towering over the group. Its eyes burned with a feral intensity, and its fangs gleamed in the darkness.

The Dogman was a terrifying sight to behold. Standing nearly seven feet tall, it was covered in thick, dark fur that seemed almost black in the dim light. Its muscular build was unmistakable, every sinew and tendon visible beneath its fur. Its eyes glowed with an unnatural light, and its elongated snout was filled with sharp, gleaming teeth.

"Get the camera on it!" Derek shouted, raising his shotgun. Sarah fumbled with her camera, trying to focus on the creature.

Back at the command center, the team watched the unfolding scene with growing horror. The drones provided a clear view of the confrontation, their infrared cameras capturing every detail.

"What are they doing?" Sheriff Walters said, his eyes glued to the screen. "They're going to get themselves killed."

The Dogman ran at them, its powerful limbs propelling it towards the group with terrifying speed. Derek fired his shotgun, the blast echoing through the forest. The shot went wide, missing the Dogman entirely.

Griffin panicked, his fingers trembling as he tried to aim his pistol. "Stay back!" he screamed, firing wildly. Bullets flew in every direction, and in the chaos, two of the team members were hit.

The Dogman's agility was astounding. It moved with a speed and grace that belied its massive size, easily dodging the wild shots from Griffin's pistol. Its eyes locked onto Derek, who was struggling to reload his shotgun.

"Stop shooting!" Sarah yelled, dropping her camera to tend to the wounded. She knelt beside one of the fallen hunters, applying pressure to a gunshot wound in his leg.

The Dogman was relentless. It swiped at Derek with a clawed hand, the force of the blow sending him sprawling to the ground. Derek's shotgun clattered away, useless.

Griffin, still firing wildly, hit another of his own team

members. The man screamed in pain as a bullet tore through his shoulder, and he fell to the ground, clutching the wound.

The Dogman, sensing an opportunity, lunged at Griffin. Its claws slashed through the air, and Griffin barely managed to dodge the attack. He stumbled backward, tripping over a root and falling hard onto the ground.

Sarah looked up, her eyes wide with terror as the Dogman turned its attention to her. She could see the intelligence in its eyes, a cold calculation as it assessed its next target.

The deputies arrived at the campground, pushing forward into the trees. "Hang on, we're coming!" Deputy Aalbers called out as they moved cautiously into the woods.

Bursting through the trees, the deputies raised their rifles and took aim at the Dogman. "Get down!" Aalbers yelled to the cryptid hunters.

The Dogman turned, its eyes locking onto the new arrivals. It roared, the sound reverberating through the forest. The deputies opened fire, their bullets finding their mark. The Dogman staggered, then retreated into the darkness, its growls fading into the night.

The command center was silent, the team processing the mess they had just witnessed. "Is everyone alright?" Sheriff

Walters asked, his voice shaky.

"Four of the cryptid hunters are down," Aalbers reported, checking on the wounded. "We need medics here, now."

"We're on it," Sheriff Walters replied, radioing for medical assistance.

Deputies Rodriguez and Fenton arrived to provide backup and keep an eye on the surrounding forest.

Derek, still on the ground and clutching his wounded arm, looked up at her. "Did you get the footage?" he asked.

Sarah, her wide open. "You're worried about that right now?"

All of them were escorted back to the campground, their bravado shattered. Shortly after, the medics arrived to tend to the injured while the deputies secured the area.

CHAPTER 57

Sheriff Walters stood next to Special Agent Miller, his face a mask of frustration and anger. "What a bunch of fools," he said, shaking his head. "Those cryptid hunters could have gotten themselves all killed. They have no idea what they're dealing with."

Miller nodded, his eyes never leaving the screens. "I agree. Their amateur tactics and recklessness could have cost more lives tonight. They could have easily scared the Dogman away from the trap or worse, gotten themselves killed."

The sheriff's frustration boiled over. "We had everything set up perfectly. The scent lures, the trap, the sensors... and then these morons show up and start shooting wildly. They could have ruined our entire operation."

Miller sighed, rubbing his temples. "Hopefully, the Dogman will enter from a different part of town. We'll keep monitoring the drones and adjust our strategy as needed. But we need to get those cryptid hunters out of here before they do any more damage."

Sheriff Walters gave a firm nod, his expression grim. He keyed his radio to Deputy Rodriguez at the campground. "Rodriguez, get the remaining cryptid hunters out of there. If they're not leaving in an ambulance, they're not staying. Make it clear—this is no longer their playground. It's not safe, and they are not coming back."

Rodriguez's voice crackled over the radio. "Glady, Sheriff. I'll handle it."

Deputy Rodriguez approached the campsite where the remaining cryptid hunters were gathered. They were visibly shaken by the recent encounter, their bravado replaced by fear and uncertainty. Derek, their leader, was nursing a wounded arm, while Sarah clutched her camera tightly, her hands trembling.

"You guys need to pack up and leave now," Jesse said firmly. "This isn't a game. There's a real dangerous creature out here, and you put yourselves and others at risk."

Derek looked up, his face pale and drawn. "But we almost had it. We got some footage of the Dogman. This could be huge for us."

Jesse shook his head. "I don't care about your footage. What matters is keeping everyone safe. You almost got yourselves killed out there. Now, pack up your gear and head out. That's an order."

Sarah glanced at Derek, then back at Jesse. "But we came all this way. We've been planning this for months."

"And now you're leaving," Jesse replied, his tone leaving no room for argument. "You will be lucky if your friends who got shot don't press charges on all of you. Pack up and get moving."

Reluctantly, the cryptid hunters began gathering their equipment. The adrenaline from their earlier encounter had worn off, leaving them with a sense of dread and realization of how close they had come to disaster.

Back at the command center, Sheriff Walters and Miller continued to monitor the drone feeds. The Dogman had retreated into the forest, but its presence was still felt. The air was charged with anticipation as they waited for any sign of movement.

"Do you think it will come back tonight?" Sheriff Walters asked, his eyes scanning the screens.

Miller shrugged. "It's hard to say. These creatures are

unpredictable. The drones will give us an early warning if it shows up again."

Sheriff Walters nodded, his jaw set in determination. "We can't let this thing slip through our fingers. We need to catch it before it hurts anyone else."

Miller agreed with a nod.

Sheriff Walters paced the command center, his frustration evident. "I just can't believe those cryptid hunters. They had no idea what they were doing. We could have lost everything tonight."

Miller watched him, understanding his anger. "They were overconfident and unprepared. It's a dangerous combination. But we need to stay focused. We can't let their stupidity derail our operation."

Sheriff Walters stopped pacing and faced Miller. "You're right. We need to stay focused. But we also need to make sure something like this doesn't happen again."

Miller nodded. "Agreed. If we don't catch it tonight, we'll have to tighten security around the trap area and maybe even issue a public warning to keep people out of the woods at night."

Sheriff Walters sighed. "It's going to be hard to keep people away, especially with all the rumors and excitement. But we have to try."

Sheriff Walters turned to the radio. "Rodriguez, what's the status at the campground?"

Rodriguez's voice came through, steady and calm. "The cryptid hunters are packing up their gear. They should be out of here soon."

"Good," Sheriff Walters replied. "Make sure they understand they can't come back. It's too dangerous."

"Will do, Sheriff," Rodriguez said. "I'll escort them out myself."

Sheriff Walters turned to Miller. "Once those cryptid hunters are gone, we can refocus on the trap and make sure everything is set up perfectly. We can't afford any more interruptions."

Miller nodded. "I'll have my team do a thorough check of all the equipment. We'll make sure everything is in working order and ready for the next sighting."

As the night wore on, Sheriff Walters and Miller stood side by side, watching the screens. The sense of urgency had not diminished, but there was also a feeling of determination. They knew they were up against a formidable opponent, but they were ready to face the challenge head-on.

"We'll get it," Sheriff Walters said quietly. "We'll catch this thing and make sure it can't hurt anyone else."

CHAPTER 58

Adam, Jerry, and Rick gathered around the screens, cups of coffee in hand. They had been watching for hours, feeling helpless as the FBI and deputies carried out the operation.

Adam sighed, staring at his coffee cup as he leaned against the counter. The aroma was rich and comforting, but it did little to calm his nerves. He poured himself another cup, hoping the caffeine would help him stay alert. He was about to take a sip when he heard footsteps approaching.

Jerry and Rick entered the makeshift kitchen area, their faces etched with worry and exhaustion. Jerry rubbed his eyes, clearly struggling to stay awake, while Rick's expression was one of frustration and restlessness.

"Long night, huh?" Adam said, offering a weak smile.

Jerry shook his head. "Yep. Figured I might as well join you for some more coffee. Maybe it'll help me stay awake."

Rick nodded in agreement. "Same here."

Adam gestured to the coffee pot. "Help yourselves. There's plenty."

Jerry poured himself a cup, followed by Rick. They all took seats around the small table, the quiet between them filled with unspoken worries.

Jerry broke the silence first. "I hate this. Sitting around, waiting for something to happen. It's like we're just waiting for bad news."

Rick nodded, his grip on his coffee mug tightening. "I know what you mean. We're here, safe and sound, while the FBI and the deputies are out there risking their lives. It doesn't feel right."

Adam took another sip of his coffee, nodding thoughtfully. "Yeah, but what can we do? We're not trained for this. We don't have the equipment or the knowledge to handle another Dogman. Especially in the woods."

Jerry sighed heavily. "You're right. It's just... hard. I feel like we should be doing something. Anything."

Rick leaned forward, his expression intense. "I know how you feel. But we have to trust that the FBI and the deputies know what they're doing. They've got the resources and the expertise. We don't."

Adam looked at his friends, seeing the same mix of frustration and helplessness in their eyes that he felt. "I keep telling myself that. But it doesn't make it any easier, just sitting here, watching the screens and waiting for updates."

As the conversation lulled, Adam found his thoughts drifting to Ruby. The end of their relationship had left a lingering sadness that he hadn't quite shaken off. He remembered the good times they had shared, the plans they had made, and the dreams that now seemed so distant.

He took a deep breath, feeling a pang of disappointment. Ruby had once been a source of support and comfort, but toward the end, their relationship had become strained and tumultuous. He missed the good times, the way her smile and laugh could lift his spirits. However, their relationship had ended, and he had to come to terms with the reality of it.

"Thinking about Ruby?" Jerry asked quietly, noticing the faraway look in Adam's eyes.

Adam nodded, giving a small, sad smile. "Yeah. Just thinking about how things ended. It's been tough."

Rick patted Adam on the shoulder. "I know it's hard, man. But you've got us. And we're here to get through this together."

Adam appreciated the gesture, feeling a bit of the weight lift from his shoulders. "Thanks, Rick. It means a lot."

The three men sat in silence for a while, the only sound the occasional clink of a coffee cup against the table. The dim light of the kitchen added to the somber mood.

Jerry finally spoke up again. "Do you think they'll catch it? The Dogman, I mean. Do you think they'll be able to stop it?"

Adam shrugged, feeling the weight of uncertainty. "I don't know. I hope so. But from what we've seen, it's not going to be easy. It wasn't last time."

Rick nodded. "And if those cryptid hunters are any indication, people are going to keep getting in the way. They've gotta be crazy for actively looking for these creatures."

Jerry frowned. "I saw the footage. Those guys were reckless. They could have gotten themselves killed. And for what? Some blurry footage to put on the internet?"

Adam sighed. "It's frustrating, alright."

The sound of a beeping monitor broke the silence,

drawing their attention back to the screens. They watched as the drones continued their surveillance, the live feeds displaying the darkened landscape of Hickory. The infrared cameras picked up the occasional movement of small animals, but there was no sign of the Dogman.

Jerry leaned forward, his eyes glued to the screen. "Look, there's movement."

Adam squinted at the screen, his heart rate quickening. "It's just a deer. But it means the drones are working. If the Dogman shows up, we'll see it."

Rick nodded, his gaze unwavering. "We just have to be patient. The team will catch it. We just have to trust them."

As they continued to watch the screens, the sense of helplessness began to ease, replaced by a shared determination. They might not be out there on the front lines, but they were still part of the effort. And that was something they could hold on to.

As the night dragged on, Special Agent Miller walked over to the small group, sensing their restlessness. He took a seat at the table and offered a reassuring smile. "How are you guys holding up?"

Adam shrugged. "We're hanging in there. Just feels like we

should be doing more."

Jerry nodded. "Yeah, it's hard just sitting here and watching."

Miller nodded understandingly. "I get it. It's tough to feel helpless. But believe me, you're doing more than you realize by being here and staying vigilant."

Rick leaned forward, his curiosity piqued. "Special Agent Miller, can you tell us more about these cryptids? We've heard bits and pieces, but what do you know about them?"

Miller hesitated for a moment, then sighed. "I can't go into too much detail, but I can share some stories."

The group leaned in, eager to hear what Miller had to say. He took a deep breath and began. "There are countless legends and reports of cryptids all over the world. Some of the most well-known ones include Bigfoot, the Loch Ness Monster, and the Chupacabra. These creatures have been part of folklore and eyewitness accounts for centuries."

Jerry's eyes widened. "Have you ever encountered any of them?"

Miller smiled faintly. "Let's just say I've been involved in a few investigations. One that stands out was a case involving a creature similar to the Chupacabra. It was in a remote part of

Texas. Livestock was being killed, and the locals were terrified. We set up surveillance, much like we're doing now, and managed to catch a glimpse of it. It was fast, cunning, and dangerous."

Adam leaned in closer. "Did you catch it?"

Miller shook his head. "No, it eluded us. But we managed to track its movements and eventually, the sightings stopped. Sometimes, these creatures seem to move on once they know they're being hunted."

Rick frowned. "Do you think that's what will happen here? That the Dogman will just move on?"

Miller looked thoughtful. "It's possible. But we have to be prepared for any outcome. The Dogman is particularly elusive and dangerous. That's why it's so important to stay focused and keep monitoring."

Sheriff Walters approached the group, his face serious. "Miller, can I have a word?"

Miller stood up, nodding to the others. "Keep your spirits up, guys. We're doing everything we can."

As Miller and Sheriff Walters moved to a quieter corner of the command center, Adam, Jerry, and Rick exchanged looks.

"You think he knows more than he's telling us?" Rick asked quietly.

Adam nodded. "Definitely. He is FBI. But I get it. There are probably lots of things he can't share with us."

Jerry sighed. "Well, at least we know we're not completely in the dark. And we've got the best people working on this."

CHAPTER 59

Special Agent Miller and Sheriff Walters were standing in front of the screens discussing their teams when suddenly one of the drones picked up a heat signature. The screen lit up with a bright red shape moving through the trees.

"We've got something," Miller said, his voice tinged with excitement. "Drone Three, northeast quadrant. It's moving toward the trap."

The room sprang into action. Special Agent Thompson, the field commander, leaned closer to the monitor, his eyes narrowing. "That's it. That's the Dogman."

Thompson grabbed his radio. "The subject is converging on the trap area. Keep your eyes focused and weapons ready. Richards, you take over from here."

Adam, Jerry, and Rick watched the operation unfold on the monitors, their hearts pounding. They could see the heat signature moving steadily through the trees, unaware of the trap waiting for it.

"Move in and engage," Richards' voice came firmly over the radio.

The agents closed in. The Dogman, sensing the encroaching threat, let out a low, deep growl. It turned its head, its glowing eyes scanning the forest.

One of the agents, a young man named Daniels, stepped too close. The Dogman struck out, its powerful limbs propelling it forward with terrifying speed. Daniels fired his weapon, but the Dogman was too quick. It struck him down with a swipe of its massive claws, sending him sprawling to the ground.

"Daniels is down!" Richards shouted. "Stay focused! Push it towards the trap!"

The team tightened their formation, using the sound of their voices and an occasional shot into the ground to drive the Dogman towards the trap. The creature snarled and snapped, its eyes glowing with a feral intensity. It was a terrifying sight: nearly seven feet tall, and brimming with raw, predatory power.

"Keep moving! Don't let it break through!" Richards barked.

The Dogman, now fully aware of the threat, tried to break through the line of agents, but they held firm. It circled, looking for an opening, its growls echoing through the forest.

Adam watched the monitors like a hawk. "Does that Dogman look a little small to you?" he asked.

Rick replied, "They're all pretty big compared to humans."

The team advanced cautiously, herding the Dogman towards the trap. The creature, realizing it was being cornered, grew more aggressive. It lunged at one of the deputies, who narrowly avoided its claws by diving to the side. The Dogman's strength and speed were incredible, and it took all of their training to keep it at bay.

"Watch out!" someone shouted as the Dogman feinted to the left, then sprang to the right. Another agent fired a shot, hitting the ground near the creature's feet. The noise startled it, and it backed off momentarily, snarling in rage.

"Don't let up! We need to keep it moving!" Richards urged.

The Dogman tried to retreat, but the team had formed a semi-circle, cutting off its escape routes. It snapped its jaws and roared, a sound that instantly sent a jolt of fear through everyone.

Richards signaled to his team to close in further. "On my count. One, two, three—move!"

The line advanced, forcing the Dogman to retreat, step by step. It swiped at the air, its massive claws slicing through the night, but the agents held their ground. The creature's movements were becoming more erratic, its frustration evident.

Daniels, still on the ground but conscious, called out weakly. "Be careful... it's damn fast."

The Dogman suddenly charged towards Richards, who stood firm, aiming his tranquilizer gun. He fired, but the Dogman dodged, the dart missing by inches. It then turned and dashed towards a thicker part of the forest.

"Don't let it get away!" Thompson yelled.

The team adjusted, moving swiftly to block its path. The Dogman skidded to a halt, snarling as it found itself facing a wall of armed agents. It was surrounded but not beaten.

With nowhere else to go, the Dogman turned and bolted straight towards the area where the trap was set. The team fell back, keeping a safe distance but maintaining their formation. The Dogman, driven by desperation and anger, didn't notice the trap as it ran headlong into it.

The trap was a sophisticated piece of equipment, designed to look like a natural part of the forest. It consisted of reinforced steel walls camouflaged with branches and leaves, and a heavy netting system that could be activated remotely.

As the Dogman ran into the trap, Richards gave the signal. "Activate the trap, now!"

Back at the command center, Thompson pressed a button on his phone, triggering the trap with a sharp metallic snap. The steel walls slammed shut, and reinforced netting shot up, ensnaring the Dogman in a web of unyielding fibers. The creature let out a furious roar, thrashing violently in a desperate attempt to break free. Within seconds, the automatic tranquilizer system activated, firing darts into its thick hide. The Dogman's struggles grew weaker as the sedative took hold, its movements slowing until it finally collapsed to the floor.

The command center erupted in a mix of cheers and sighs of relief. Adam, Jerry, and Rick exchanged looks of disbelief and triumph. They had done it. They had captured the Dogman.

Richards radioed back to the command center. "The Dogman is down, secured in the trap. We've got it."

Sheriff Walters approached Miller, a look of relief on his face. "They did it. They actually did it."

Miller nodded, his expression relieved. "Yes, we did."

Adam, Jerry, and Rick stood nearby, their expressions a mix of excitement and apprehension.

Miller shook his head. "This is just the beginning. We've captured it, but now we need to transport it to a secure facility."

Sheriff Walters turned to the group. "For now, let's focus on securing the area and making sure everyone is safe. We've accomplished something incredible tonight, but we need to stay on our guard."

As the team worked to secure the command center and transport the Dogman to a secure facility, a sense of accomplishment filled the air. They had faced an extraordinary challenge and emerged victorious. But they knew that the journey ahead was still fraught with uncertainty and danger.

"Thank God," Adam said quietly, a sense of awe in his voice. "Did anyone happen to notice if it was male or female? It looked rather small to me."

Rick clapped him on the back. "No. But it could just be

younger than the one we killed."

Adan nodded slowly. "Yeah, could be."

CHAPTER 60

The operation had been a success, but the work was far from over. The FBI truck, a reinforced transport vehicle, was parked outside the command center, its engine idling softly. Inside the truck, the Dogman lay still on the steel floor.

Special Agent Thompson stood beside the truck, issuing orders to his team as they prepared for the next phase of the mission. "We need to secure everything and make sure we're ready for transport. This thing is dangerous, and we can't afford any mistakes."

His team, all seasoned agents, moved with precision and purpose, checking their gear and loading it into the truck. They knew the journey ahead would be critical, and they couldn't let their guard down for a moment.

Inside the command center, Special Agent Miller walked over to Adam, Jerry and Rick, his face serious but calm. "We're about to transport the Dogman to our secure facility. It's going to be a long trip, and we need to make sure everything is in order."

Adam nodded. "Do you think it'll stay sedated?"

Miller sighed. "We've administered a strong dose of tranquilizers, but we can't take any chances. That's why we're being extra cautious."

Jerry looked at Miller, his curiosity piqued. "What happens next? Once you get it to your facility?"

Miller hesitated for a moment before answering. "We have a specialized containment unit designed for animals like this. Our team of scientists and experts will study it, try to learn more about them. We need to know its origins, its capabilities, and most importantly, how to prevent any future incidents."

Special Agent Thompson entered the command center, having finished the preparations outside. He approached Sheriff Walters and his deputies, extending a hand. "Sheriff, I want to thank you and your team for your cooperation and bravery. We couldn't have done this without you."

Sheriff Walters shook his hand firmly. "We were just doing our job, but thank you. And I have to say, you and your team did an incredible job out there."

Thompson turned to Adam, Jerry, and Rick. "And to you three, thank you for your insights and your help. Your knowledge and vigilance were invaluable."

Adam, slightly taken aback, nodded. "We just wanted to help keep our town safe."

Jerry added, "We're just glad it worked out."

Rick smiled. "Just make sure that thing stays locked up."

Outside, Special Agent Thompson and his team had finished gathering their gear. Thompson approached the truck, checking the cage one last time. The Dogman was still sedated, its breathing slow and heavy. "We're ready to roll. Everyone stay sharp and stick to the plan," he said to his team.

Miller, standing beside the truck, nodded. "We'll escort you as far as the county line. After that, you're on your own. Stay in constant contact and update us on any changes."

Thompson acknowledged the orders and gave a final nod to his team. "Alright, let's move out."

The transport vehicle began to roll forward, flanked by two FBI SUVs. The convoy moved slowly and carefully, the agents focused on the road ahead. The streets of Hickory were quiet as the sun started creeping over the horizon.

Adam, Jerry, and Rick stood together, watching as the transport vehicle drove away. They had been through a lot, but they were thankful that the threat to the townsfolk was finally over.

CHAPTER 61

Eddie's house was a humble, single-story structure on the outskirts of Hickory, nestled near the edge of the forest. The first rays of sunrise began to filter through the trees, casting a golden glow over the town.

They had just finished making love and lay in bed, their breathing still heavy, their bodies entwined. Ruby, her head resting on Eddie's chest, felt a rare sense of contentment wash over her. For a moment, the guilt and stress of betraying Adam seemed far away, replaced by the comforting rhythm of Eddie's heartbeat.

The soft light of dawn illuminated the room, giving everything a warm, serene quality. Ruby traced lazy circles on Eddie's chest, savoring the quiet moments. The world outside seemed calm, the new day bringing a sense of hope and renewal.

Eddie broke the silence with a smug grin. "I bet Adam's regretting losing you right about now," he said, his tone dripping with arrogance.

Ruby's contentment vanished instantly, replaced by a surge of disgust. She pulled away from him, sitting up and glaring. "Why would you bring him up now? Can't you just let it go?"

Eddie chuckled, not bothered by her anger. "Come on, Ruby. You know it's a rush, knowing I took you from him. He must be losing his mind."

Ruby felt her stomach churn with a mix of anger and revulsion. "You're unbelievable," she snapped. "Is that all you care about? That you 'won'?"

Eddie shrugged, his smirk never fading. The truth was, he didn't have the emotional depth to actually care for someone. He enjoyed having Ruby around to clean up, have sex with, and boost his ego. "What can I say? I enjoy the victory. I am pretty sure you did, too."

Ruby turned her back to him as she got dressed. "You're a pig."

Eddie sighed, sitting up and stretching. "Lighten up, Ruby.

I'm just having some fun." He got out of bed and pulled on a pair of shorts. "I'm going to grab a drink."

He padded out of the bedroom, the creaky wooden floorboards announcing his every step. In the kitchen, Eddie opened the fridge, the cold air a stark contrast to the warmth of the bed he had just left. He grabbed a bottle of water and took a long drink, his mind wandering back to Ruby. Despite their rocky relationship, he enjoyed the thrill of being with her, mostly because of how it annoyed Adam.

As he stood there, lost in thought, he heard footsteps on the porch and the sound of the old wooden planks creaking under the weight. Eddie frowned, setting the bottle down on the counter. The sound made him think immediately that a burglar was trying to get in.

"They've picked the wrong damn house," he said to himself. Feeling a surge of false bravado, Eddie decided to confront whoever it was. He reached for the doorknob and hesitated, an instant chill running down his spine. Taking a deep breath, he turned the knob and yanked the door open, stepping out onto the porch.

"Who the hell's out here?" Eddie barked, trying to sound tough. He squinted in the low light but saw nothing at first. Then, a shadow shifted, and Eddie's heart did backflips. There, crouched on the porch, was a massive, hulking figure. Its eyes glowed with a malevolent light, and Eddie gasped.

Before he could react, the Dogman ran forward with terrifying speed. Eddie barely had time to register the movement before the creature's claws raked across his chest, sending him sprawling backward. He hit the floor hard, the wind knocked out of him, blood spreading rapidly across his chest.

Ruby was in the bathroom when she heard the commotion, her heart pounding. "Eddie?" she called out, her voice laced with unease. When there was no response, she quickly washed her hands and stepped out, her pulse increasing as she moved down the hallway.

"Eddie, quit playing around!" she called again as she stepped into the kitchen. The sounds of a struggle came from the living room, and her fear intensified. "What's going on?"

As she approached the living room, she saw Eddie lying on the floor, blood pooling around him. Hunched over him, its eyes glowing with rage, was the Dogman.

Ruby screamed as the creature turned her gaze on her, lips curling back in a snarl.

"Eddie!" she shrieked, rushing forward. The Dogman met her charge with a brutal swipe of her massive claws, sending

Ruby crashing into the wall. The impact knocked the breath from her lungs, and she crumpled to the floor, pain radiating from the deep gashes in her side.

Eddie, fighting through his own agony, tried to crawl toward her. "Run... Ruby... get out..." he gasped, his vision blurring. But the Dogman was upon him again, her powerful jaws closing around his head. Eddie screamed as she lifted him off the ground, shaking him like a ragdoll.

Ruby, her vision swimming with tears and pain, watched in horror as the Dogman savaged Eddie. She knew she had to do something, but her body refused to cooperate. The room spun, her limbs heavy and unresponsive.

With a final, brutal shake, the Dogman tossed Eddie's lifeless body aside. She turned her attention back to Ruby, her eyes burning with cold, unrelenting hatred. Ruby tried to crawl away, her hands scrabbling at the floor, but the creature was too fast.

In two strides, the Dogman reached her, claws clamping around her ankle. Ruby screamed, the sound piercing the night, but there was no one to hear her. The Dogman dragged her across the floor, grip like iron. She kicked and struggled, but it was no use.

Desperate, Ruby reached for a lamp on a nearby table,

swinging it at the creature with all her strength. The lamp shattered against the Dogman's head, but she barely flinched. With a snarl, she lifted Ruby off the ground, claws digging deep as blood dripped onto the floor.

Ruby's screams echoed through the house as the Dogman sank her teeth into Ruby's neck. The pain was excruciating, her vision darkening at the edges. She felt her strength draining away, her body growing cold.

As the darkness closed in, Ruby's last thought was of Adam. She had wronged him, betrayed him, and now she realized he had been right all along—the Dogman was real. Very real. She was paying the ultimate price for her disbelief. In her final moments, she hoped Adam would find a way to survive and protect himself from the monster that had taken her life.

The Dogman lowered herself over the bodies, her powerful jaws tearing into flesh, feeding with primal efficiency. Blood pooled across the floor beneath her as muscle and sinew were ripped away, devoured in great, ravenous gulps. The scent of death hung in the air, but she paid no mind. She ate until her hunger dulled, until the primal need to consume faded into the background.

Lifting her head, licking the remnants of her meal from her fangs, she noticed the sunlight filtering more brightly through the trees and into the house. The realization made her ears flick back, instincts warning that she had lingered too long. With a final glance at the carnage left behind, the Dogman turned and bolted, disappearing through the ruined doorway and into the thinning shadows of the retreating night.

EPILOGUE

After a soothing shower, Adam was just about to settle into bed. The hot water had helped ease some of the ache in his muscles, but his mind was still processing everything that had happened. It had been a long and grueling night, filled with fear, adrenaline, and a desperate hope that the nightmare was finally over. He had checked the locks on his doors and windows twice before finally allowing himself to relax. Just as he was about to drift off to sleep, a loud knock on his front door jolted him awake.

He frowned, glancing at the clock. It was almost 9a.m. Adam quickly pulled on a pair of jeans and a T-shirt, hurrying to the door. He peered through the peephole and was surprised to see the sheriff standing on his porch.

"Sheriff?" Adam said as he opened the door. "What are you

doing here?"

Sheriff Walters's face was drawn and weary, dark circles under his eyes betraying his own exhaustion. "Adam, can I come in?" he asked, his voice somber.

Adam nodded, stepping aside to let the sheriff enter.

"Of course. Is everything alright?"

The sheriff sighed heavily, removing his hat and running a hand through his hair. "I wish I could say yes, but I'm afraid I have some bad news. I just came from Eddie's house."

The mention of Eddie's name caused a knot to form in Adam's stomach. He felt a sudden sense of dread. "What happened?"

Sheriff Walters took a deep breath, meeting Adam's eyes. "Adam, Eddie and Ruby are dead. It looks like they were killed by the Dogman."

The words hit Adam like a physical blow. He staggered back, leaning against the wall for support. "What? How... when?"

The sheriffs' expression was grim. "About an hour and a half ago. A neighbor heard screaming and called it in. By the time my deputies got there, it was too late. The scene was a mess."

Adam felt his heart pounding in his chest, a mix of shock, grief, and sadness. Ruby, despite everything that had happened between them, had been a significant part of his life. The realization that she was gone, brutally killed, was almost too much to bear.

"Ruby…" Adam said, his voice barely above a whisper. "I can't believe it. Are you sure it was a Dogman?"

Sheriff Walters nodded. "The injuries match. Claw marks, bite wounds."

Adam's mind was a whirlwind of thoughts.

"Sheriff," Adam asked urgently, "the Dogman we captured, was it a male or female?"

"It was a male," the sheriff replied.

Adam's expression darkened. "Oh no. When we talked to Chris, he mentioned seeing pronounced nipples. The Dogman outside my house was female too. When they captured the one this morning, I thought it looked a little small. It didn't seem as big as the one I saw the other night."

Sheriff Walters' eyes narrowed. "Are you saying there's more than one?"

Adam nodded, his voice steady despite the rising panic. "Yes. The one they caught was small, a juvenile, I'm guessing. It was under sedation in the FBI cage an hour and a half ago, so it could not have killed Eddie and Ruby. The one that killed them... I'm betting is the mother. I can't prove it, of course, but that's what my gut says."

The sheriff's leaned against the wall as the gravity of the situation sunk in. "My God... I was too tired to realize the timing. I thought we had it under control."

Adam clenched his fists, anger and determination flaring within him. "Shit. You need to call the FBI. This isn't over. If I'm right, we're now dealing with a mother who has lost her child. She's not just a wild animal; she's a predator with an even bigger purpose now."

The sheriff placed a reassuring hand on Adam's shoulder.

"We'll do everything we can to stop her, Adam. But right now, you need to stay inside and get some rest. Don't go out there alone. I will alert the FBI.

Adam nodded, his mind still reeling from the news. "I understand, Sheriff. I just... I can't believe Ruby's gone..."

The sheriff sighed, his expression softening. "I know this

is hard, Adam. Get some rest and call me when you're ready."

As the sheriff left, Adam closed the door and leaned against it, his mind a whirlwind of emotions. He felt a deep sense of loss for Ruby, mixed with a burning anger at the creature that had taken her life. He knew he had to stay strong, to protect those who were still alive.

He walked through his house, checking the locks and windows once more. The memories of the past few weeks flooded his mind, the constant fear and the relentless pursuit of the Dogman. He knew now that they were facing a more formidable enemy, one driven by rage and a primal instinct to protect its young.

Adam made his way to the kitchen and poured himself a whiskey, hoping it would help him fall asleep.

He thought about Ruby, her smile, and the times they had shared. Despite their recent troubles, he had cared for her deeply. The guilt of not being able to protect her ate at him.

Adam grabbed his phone and dialed Jerry's number. When he answered groggily, Adam took a deep breath and said, "It's not over, bud. They captured the wrong one. Mama's still out there, and she'll be coming for her baby."

ABOUT THE AUTHOR

 Luka T. Jacobs, an author from the picturesque Illawarra region south of Sydney, Australia, is passionate about cryptids like Sasquatch and Dogman. She lives there with her partner and their dog, Finnigan.

Luka's love for animals and adventure fuels her storytelling. With a background in Graphic Design and Art, she adds a unique visual flair to her work. An avid traveler and explorer, she draws inspiration from the wild, eager to share her imaginative worlds with readers.

Luka T. Jacobs

Stay connected and join the conversation! Follow me on Facebook to interact and share your thoughts, explore my books on Amazon, and visit my website for more information about my works and upcoming releases.

FB: **https://www.facebook.com/lukatjacobs**

A: **https://amazon.com/author/lukatjacobs**

W: **http://www.LukaTJacobs.com**

JOIN CRYPTID HORROR CENTRAL

Join my email list and get first access to new releases and download my FREE short story "The Dogman of Coldwater Creek".

WWW.LUKATJACOBS.COM

Dear Reader,

Thank you for diving into my book amidst a sea of choices, it truly means the world to me.

If you enjoyed the story, I'd love it if you shared your experience with others and left a review. As an independent author, your voice helps bring these tales to life for more readers, and every recommendation makes a tremendous impact.

Thank you again for joining me on this journey.
I'm so grateful to have you as a reader!

SNEAK PEEK: NIGHT OF THE DOGMAN: VENGEANCE

The headlights of the Audi pierced through the darkened landscape as David and Sheila journeyed home on Route 60. The day had been long, filled with shopping in Springfield—her favorite pastime. David, ever the dutiful husband, trailed behind her in silence, his thoughts elsewhere as she gleefully spent his money. He had grown accustomed to her constant demands and complaints, so much so that her voice became little more than background noise, easily tuned out. Tonight was no different.

They were nearing Willow Springs, and the clock on the dashboard glowed 9:38 PM. Sheila was in mid-rant, her words sharp and accusatory, but David's responses were automatic—"Yes, dear," he mumbled whenever she paused for breath, not really hearing what she said. His mind wandered, contemplating the trap of his marriage and the bitter reality that leaving would cost him everything he had worked for as a successful Orthodontist. She held no respect for him or his money. And though he longed to be free, he knew the consequences would be devastating. At least they had never wanted kids, he mused.

As they approached a dark corner, he turned to her, offering a half-hearted reply to whatever she had been complaining about. But her voice suddenly cut through the air with a scream: "Watch out!"

David shifted his gaze to the road just in time to see something dark and hulking appear out of nowhere, clipping the front right of the car with a sickening thud. He screeched to a stop, the Audi halting on the gravel shoulder. His pulse raced as he tried to comprehend what had just happened.

"What the hell are you doing? You could have killed me, you idiot!" Sheila's voice was shrill, her fear masked by anger.

"It was a dog… or something. I think I hit someone's dog," he mumbled, already opening the door.

"Who cares? It's dark and freezing out here. Just leave it!"

But he couldn't escape the notion that he needed to check. If it was still on the road, it could cause another accident. Ignoring her protests, David stepped out, the frigid night wind biting at his skin. The only light came from his cell phone as he cautiously moved toward the rear of the car, scanning the area. His breath fogged in the chill, and the stillness of the night seemed to close in around him.

There, lying in the road just behind the car, he saw it. At first sight, it appeared to be a dog—mangy, large, and pitifully injured. It was dragging itself along the asphalt, its legs twisted at unnatural angles. His heart ached at the sight; he had always loved dogs, but Sheila would never allow one in their home. Slowly, he walked closer, the beam of his phone light trembling while he absorbed the scene.

But as the light fully illuminated the creature, a chill deeper than the night air seeped into his bones. This "dog" differed completely from anything he had ever seen. It was enormous, its body grotesque and malformed. Then it stopped moving.

David watched, paralyzed, as the monster rose—unfolding itself, he thought numbly. As it did, a sickening sound filled the night, like the cracking of bones, each snap echoing in his ears and making his stomach drop. It stood on two legs, towering over him at nearly eight feet tall. The once limp form had transformed into a monstrous figure, covered in thick, matted fur that clung to its powerful frame. Its legs were muscular and bent like a dog's, ending in clawed, canine feet. The creature's hands were overly large, with elongated fingers that ended in razor-sharp claws, perfect for tearing flesh.

Its face was a nightmarish visage of pure beast—a long,

lupine snout with rows of gleaming, sharp teeth, and eyes that glowed with a cold, calculating focus. A pair of pointed ears twitched as it locked its gaze onto his, its eyes narrowing with an intent that made his skin crawl. Then, to his horror, it cocked its head and smirked, the expression chillingly human on its otherwise monstrous face.

Completely oblivious to the horror outside, Sheila's impatient voice cut through David's terror, her complaints growing frantic as she berated him for leaving her in the cold.

The creature's attention shifted past David, locking onto the car. Its eyes shone with a predatory hunger as it licked its chops, the smirk twisting into something far more sinister.

His paralysis broke, and he spun around, heart thudding in his ears. Just as he was about to take a step, excruciating agony surged through him as the beast leaped onto his back, its claws sinking deep into his shoulders and raking down his spine, tearing through flesh and muscle. His screams pierced the night, a raw, desperate sound that was abruptly cut short when the monster yanked him back up with inhuman strength.

With terrifying force, it slammed him against the car, causing excruciating pain throughout his body. Some of the broken ribs punctured his lung, and he gasped, choking on blood as it filled his mouth. His breath came in ragged, shallow bursts, each one more labored than the last.

The Dogman wasn't finished.

It clawed viciously at his chest, ripping through skin and muscle, leaving deep, jagged wounds that oozed dark blood. The pain was unbearable, but his screams had turned to wet gurgles as blood choked his throat. He collapsed to the ground, dazed and barely conscious, his vision dimming as the creature loomed over him, emitting a deep, rumbling growl that reverberated through his entire body—a sound of pure, merciless menace.

Every breath he took was agony, his body rapidly failing as the blood loss and internal injuries overwhelmed him. He could feel his life slipping away, his strength fading gradually, as the beast watched with dark, wicked eyes.

Sheila's voice, once sharp with impatience, was now frantic and tinged with fear. She hadn't yet seen the full extent of the horror outside, but she had heard David's screams. The creature had already shifted its attention to the car, the shine of its eyes revealing its hunger as it approached the passenger side.

She didn't notice the beast until it was right beside the car, its blood-soaked claws scraping the metal as it placed a massive hand on the door. The noise of nails screeching against the steel made her breath hitch in her throat. She gradually shifted, her eyes drawn to the dark, crimson-streaked talons that rested on the window. For a split second, confusion clouded her mind—*what in the hell is that*?

But when she followed the line of the creature's arm upward and her gaze locked onto the face looming outside the glass, terror surged through her like an electric shock. The Dogman's hideous snout was inches from the window, its breath fogging up the glass with each exhale. Its eyes were locked onto hers, gleaming with malevolent intelligence that sent ice through her veins.

Before Sheila could even scream, the creature acted. With supernatural strength, it drove its fist through the window; the glass shattering in an explosion of shards that glinted like deadly stars in the dim light. The suddenness of the attack robbed her of her breath, leaving her frozen in shock. Then, with deliberate slowness, it reached inside, its claws closing around her arm like a vice.

She finally found her voice, but the scream that tore from her throat was the cry of pure panic. She attempted to fight, thrashing against the creature's grip, her nails clawing at its leathery skin, but it was futile. The Dogman's strength was overwhelming, its grip unyielding. With a nauseating crunch, it yanked her out of the car, her body hitting the ground with a bone-jarring thud.

David, still battling to stay conscious, heard Sheila's screams turn into gurgling cries as the creature's claws slashed through her flesh. The sound was a surreal symphony of tearing skin and splintering bone, each note driving deeper into his fading awareness. Her warm blood sprayed across the pavement, painting the night in a gruesome display of violence.

As the darkness crept closer to him, David's last sight was the Dogman standing over Sheila's broken body, its muzzle slick with her blood. The creature looked up, its gaze meeting his, and in that moment, David saw something that made his blood run cold—a twisted satisfaction in its eyes, as if it reveled in the horror it had unleashed.

THE HAIRS ON THE BACK OF YOUR NECK WILL NEVER LAY FLAT AGAIN.

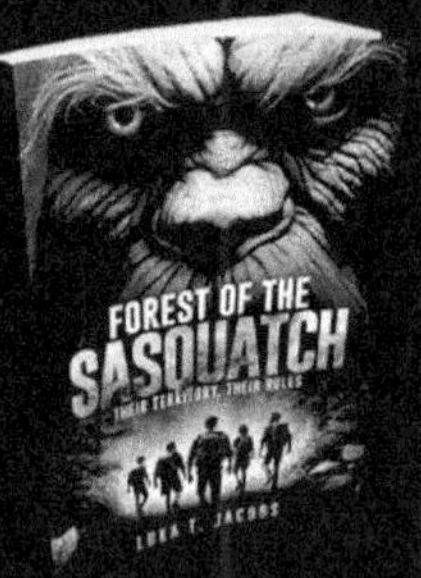

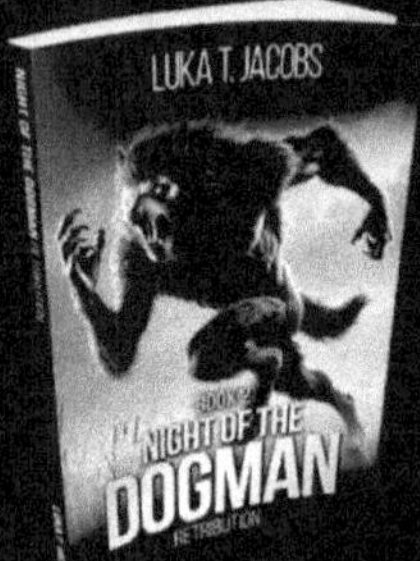

CURRENT TITLES

AS AT JAN 25

kindleunlimited